**It would be nice to be part of a team again, after four years of patchy locum work as his brother had grown steadily more dependent.**

He'd taken time out to help his parents, but he'd missed it, missed the camaraderie, the belonging.

Nick wanted to belong again, and from what he'd seen so far, he'd be welcomed with open arms by the other practice members.

And then there was Ellie.

Ellie, with her long dark hair, gray-green eyes that showed every emotion and that wickedly dry sense of humor. Not to mention a curvy, womanly body that made him ache to wrap her up in his arms and kiss her senseless.

No, that would be he who'd be senseless, because it wasn't just her eyes and her wit and her lush, beautiful body. It was her three very small children, all part of the same package, and he wanted nothing to do with it.

*Liar.*

Dear Reader,

Have you ever done something that's had repercussions for the rest of your life? We can all make mistakes, but when the consequences are life changing, we have to find a way to live with it.

Nick made a reckless decision when he was seventeen that's changed his life forever. It doesn't mean he can't have a successful career or a fulfilling life, but marriage and a family are not for him. He's lost Sam, the brother he'd cared for for years, and now he needs peace and time to heal. Then he meets Ellie, and slowly he begins to see what he's missing. Is he brave enough to try for all the things he's been denying himself? Can he convince her to try, too?

But Ellie's had a tough time, and now her priority has to be her three little children. There's no room in that life for Nick—or is there? Can she turn back time and give him what he thought he'd lost forever, and by doing so find happiness for herself and her children?

Oh, and there's Rufus, Nick's brother's dog, the catalyst and heart stealer…

I hope you enjoy them all!

*Caroline* x

# TEMPTED BY THE SINGLE MOM

---

## CAROLINE ANDERSON

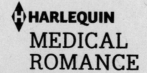

**H**HARLEQUIN

MEDICAL
ROMANCE

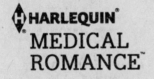

# HARLEQUIN®
## MEDICAL
## ROMANCE™

Recycling programs
for this product may
not exist in your area.

ISBN-13: 978-1-335-14933-6

Tempted by the Single Mom

Copyright © 2020 by Caroline Anderson

This edition published by arrangement with Harlequin Books S.A.

For questions and comments about the quality of this book,
please contact us at CustomerService@Harlequin.com.

Harlequin Enterprises ULC
22 Adelaide St. West, 40th Floor
Toronto, Ontario M5H 4E3, Canada
www.Harlequin.com

**Printed in U.S.A.**

**Caroline Anderson** is a matriarch, writer, armchair gardener, unofficial tearoom researcher and eater of lovely cakes. Not necessarily in that order! What Caroline loves: her family. Her friends. Reading. Writing contemporary love stories. Hearing from readers. Walks by the sea with coffee/ice cream/ cake thrown in! Torrential rain. Sunshine in spring/ autumn. What Caroline hates: losing her pets. Fighting with her family. Cold weather. Hot weather. Computers. Clothes shopping. Caroline's plans: keep smiling and writing!

### Books by Caroline Anderson

### Harlequin Medical Romance

#### *Hope Children's Hospital*
*One Night, One Unexpected Miracle*

#### *Yoxburgh Park Hospital*

*From Christmas to Eternity*
*The Secret in His Heart*
*Risk of a Lifetime*
*Their Meant-to-Be Baby*
*The Midwife's Longed-For Baby*
*Bound by Their Babies*
*Their Own Little Miracle*
*A Single Dad to Heal Her Heart*
*From Heartache to Forever*

Visit the Author Profile page
at Harlequin.com for more titles.

I have many people to thank, not least my editor for her endless patience. Sheila, you are a star.

Also Juno, who's looked after us for very many years through many trials and tribulations. Thank you for your kindness and support.

And last but not least, thanks also to my long-suffering husband, John, who must surely be sick of me saying, 'We can't do that. I have to write my book…'

# CHAPTER ONE

WHY? WHY TODAY, when she was already running late before she'd even started, did someone have to make it even worse?

She glared at the car reversing neatly into the one remaining doctors' space—a car she didn't recognise, and she'd never seen the driver, either. He certainly wasn't one of their doctors, so whoever he was he had no business parking there.

Didn't seem to bother him. He either didn't know, or didn't care, but he flashed her a smile as he got out of the car, then locked it and headed for the surgery without a backward glance.

Who did he think he was? Cocky, arrogant—argh! There weren't words for what she felt. The expensive car, the confident stride, the easy charm—not to mention the insanely good looks. Clearly a man for whom everything had always gone his way. Well, not now.

Whoever he was—probably a drug rep—he was about to get his comeuppance.

Still fuming, she reversed into the last available space in the car park, not really wide enough but doable—or it would have been, if she hadn't been so cross.

She heard the scrape, closed her eyes and breathed, then shuffled the car slightly further from the offending wall, squeezed out of the ridiculously narrow gap she'd left herself, slammed the door and headed across the car park.

Seriously, could today *get* any worse? Well, his could. If he was still in Reception—

He was. He was chatting to the receptionist, leaning forward engagingly as he spoke, and that easy charm was obviously working on Katie, which just infuriated her more. His hands were shoved casually into the pockets of immaculately cut trousers that fitted his neat, strong hips to perfection. Of course they did. They wouldn't dare do anything else.

She eyed his shoulders, broad and yet not heavy, the legs strong and straight below firm, taut buttocks. He probably worked out in a fancy gym somewhere. You didn't get a neat, sexy bottom like that by accident.

She dragged her eyes up to head height.

'You've parked in a doctor's space,' she said

crisply to his back, keeping a lid on her temper with difficulty, and he straightened up and turned towards her, that infuriating smile still on his face.

'Yes, I—'

'I know parking's tight, but that is just not on. There was another space, so why not park there yourself? Or anywhere else, frankly! Or was that the only space big enough for your ego? Thanks to you I've scraped my car, I'm now ten minutes late and I've got patients waiting!'

An eyebrow rose a fraction. Over his shoulder she could see Katie gesturing wildly, but she ignored her and stood her ground, and he shook his head slowly.

'Maybe you need to get up earlier,' he murmured, and she stifled the urge to growl at him.

'And maybe you need to learn to read!'

'Ellie! Dr Kendal!' Katie chipped in, getting to her feet and looking even more flustered, and his eyebrow went up a little further, a lazy smile now playing around his aggravatingly beautiful mouth.

'I think we'd better start again,' he said, holding out his hand, the smile tugging at his lips. 'It's a pleasure to meet you, Dr Kendal. I'm Nick Cooper. *Dr* Nick Cooper.'

The new—and desperately needed—member of their team.

Brilliant.

*Why didn't the ground just open up and swallow her?*

He had to stifle his laugh.

Her jaw sagged, and for a second she was speechless. Then she shook her head, mumbled what could have been an apology and fled through the staff door as Katie opened it, her face flaming.

He dropped his hand back to his side, shrugged and smiled at the receptionist who was looking horrified and fascinated all at once.

'So, that's Dr Kendal,' he murmured, vaguely intrigued.

'Yes. Ellie. I'm so sorry, she's normally lovely. I don't know what's got into her.'

He pulled a face and walked through the door into the back of Reception, closing it behind himself. 'I do. I took the last doctor's space, and now she's scraped her car. Oops. If I'd known who she was I would have moved, but I didn't have a clue.'

'She's only part-time, so if she wasn't on duty when you came for your interviews you wouldn't have met her—and she does normally walk. You weren't to know.'

He nodded. 'No. Ah, well. I have no doubt we'll have time to catch up later.'

Katie gestured towards the other doorway, still looking flustered. 'Come in and I'll introduce you to the admin team, and I'm sure Dr Gallagher will be out in a minute to talk to you. I've let her know you're here.'

She led the way, and he followed her into the office and scanned it for any sign of his fiery new colleague, but she'd gone.

Pity. Never mind. He was here all day, there was time, and he could look forward to what was bound to be an interesting conversation...

*Why had she done that?*

Torn him to pieces without even giving him a chance to speak? And if he'd been a patient, he would have been well within his rights to complain. No, it was even better than that. He was a colleague, her senior, and she'd just hurled abuse at him in their first interaction.

Marvellous. Just marvellous.

Not that he'd been exactly polite himself, telling her to get up earlier. She'd been up before half five as it was to do the laundry, and if Maisie hadn't been a diva and Evie hadn't needed her nappy changed again and Oscar hadn't lost one of his shoes and then had a meltdown, she wouldn't have been late and then none of this would have happened.

She felt her eyes prickle, and clamped her jaw shut hard, blinking furiously as she closed her consulting room door behind her and leant against it. It could have been worse. There could have been a whole bunch of patients in Reception, so at least she hadn't had an audience while she'd made a total fool of herself.

'Breathe,' she said softly, and closed her eyes, sucking in a long, slow breath through her nose and out through her mouth. In…and out… In…and out—

The quiet tap on the door made her jump, and she leapt away from it and wrenched it open, to find herself face to face with her worst nightmare, no doubt coming to tear her apart in private. Well, it was certainly justified, and he probably hated her already.

Or maybe not…

'Katie thought you'd want this,' he said quietly, holding out a mug of tea without a trace of a smile, and she stared at it suspiciously.

*Beware of strangers bearing gifts…*

'Why are you bringing me a peace offering? I'm the one who should be apologising—or have you slipped something into it?'

His mouth twitched. 'Don't tempt me,' he

murmured, and gave her a wry smile. 'It's not a peace offering. Katie was about to bring it to you, and I suggested I do it. I thought we could do with clearing the air.'

She took it from him with fingers that weren't quite steady, then made herself meet his eyes. He held her gaze, his searching, thoughtful, the smile gone now. She was quite glad she didn't know what he was thinking...

She felt her shoulders drop in defeat. 'Look, I'm sorry, I didn't know who you were, which is no excuse whatsoever, I know that, but—' She broke off, still mortified and wondering if there was any way she could rescue the situation. 'I hadn't realised you were coming in today, I thought you'd be starting on Monday, so I wasn't expecting you, I didn't recognise you, and then you took the last reserved space, and as if that wasn't enough I scraped my car parking by the wall, which was just the icing on the cake—'

'Ellie, breathe! It's OK. Forget it. You're right, I *am* starting on Monday, I'm just having an induction today, learning the ropes a bit, finding my feet before I start. I guess nobody told you. And I'm sorry I took your parking place, but Lucy told me to park there because you usually walk to work. Obviously not today.'

'No. I should have been, I nearly always do, but I got—held up,' she said, for want of a better way of putting it.

'So it seems. Parking's tight, isn't it? Lucy said it's a regular occurrence with the building work going on.'

She nodded, sighing with relief because he had every right to be unreasonable about this. 'It is, but they should be finished soon and the builders' vans will be gone, and not a moment too soon. Look, I'm sorry, can we do this later? I don't mean to be rude—again—but I do have patients waiting and I'm already on the drag.'

'Of course. And I'm sorry about the parking—and your car.'

'Don't be sorry. You had every right to park there, as it turns out, and I massively overreacted. And thank you for the tea. I haven't had time for one today.'

His eyes softened at the corners, that flickering smile sending strange little shivers through her body. 'My pleasure,' he murmured. 'We'll catch up later.' His lips twitched again. 'You can teach me to read, and I can teach you to tell the time.'

She rolled her eyes. He might have forgiven her, but he clearly wasn't going to let it drop.

'Oh, I can tell the time,' she told him wryly.

'I was up at five twenty-seven, for what it's worth.'

A silent ah, and he backed out, fingers waggling. 'Better not hold you up any more, then. I'll see you later.'

She nodded, and the door closed softly behind him.

Shaking her head and wishing she could wind the clock back, she put the tea down, washed her hands and fired up her computer, her mind refusing to let go of that lazy, sexy, fleeting smile.

Stupid. She was nearly twenty minutes late now, and it would have a knock-on effect on the rest of the day. She didn't have time to daydream, and particularly not about a man who probably practised his smile in the mirror!

'Get a grip, Ellie,' she told herself, took a gulp of her tea and pressed the button to call her first patient.

Predictably she finished her morning surgery late, checked some results and wrote two referral letters and then, just because why not, when she went upstairs to their temporary staff room to make herself a coffee and eat the lunch she'd hastily thrown together at crazy o'clock, Nick was in there alone.

Time to eat humble pie again...

He looked up from the paperwork scattered on the table in front of him, and his unbelievably blue, improbably beautiful eyes locked on hers with that clear, steady gaze that she was beginning to find unnerving.

'OK?'

She laughed. Was she? Probably. 'I'll live. People don't normally die of embarrassment. Have they abandoned you?'

'They're all busy. I'm fine. I'm reading through a pile of stuff they gave me and I was sort of hoping you'd come in so we could start again.'

'No need, Nick, it's fine, and I think I've probably said enough to last a lifetime. Can we just drop it? I'm not normally so inexcusably rude.'

'I'm sure you're not, but you were hassled and I was in your space. And you'd just trashed your car.'

She shrugged and headed for the kettle. 'It's hardly trashed, it barely shows, and I still shouldn't have been so rude. You could have been anyone.'

Though how anyone else would have been worse than the new partner it was hard to imagine.

He got to his feet and headed over to where she was standing, moving with a lithe, easy grace—and a slight wince? 'Let's start again. I'm Nick.'

'And I'm Ellie.'

She took the hand he was holding out to her, and as his fingers wrapped around her hand she felt warmth and reassurance and strength. And about a million volts. She dropped it like a hot potato, and he switched on the kettle and settled back against the worktop edge, legs crossed at the ankle, arms folded, sex appeal pouring off his perfectly honed body in waves.

*Why did he have to be so darned sexy?*

'I'll get you a drink, you eat your lunch,' he said, that smile flickering again. 'And while you do that, you can tell me why you were up at five twenty-seven.'

She rolled her eyes, handed him her empty mug and ripped the lid off her lunch box, retreating to the other side of the table for a bit of much-needed distance.

'Coffee, please, white, no sugar. And since you asked, it was nothing unusual, I'm often up that early. I put the washing on, hung out the load which had done overnight, showered, dressed, hung out the second load, got the kids up, finally got them dressed after the usual arguments, we had breakfast, then Maisie had another strop because her best dress was on the line, Oscar lost a shoe and then had a meltdown and wouldn't put his other shoes on, and Evie did a poo so I had to change her nappy, by which time Oscar had taken his shoes off again and hidden them, and Maisie was changing her dress for the third time. So, just another day at the office, really.'

He put the coffee down in front of her, his eyes wide and brimming with something that could have been sympathy if it hadn't been for the laughter fighting its way to the top.

'Ouch,' he said softly, sitting down again and propping his elbows on the table as he held her eyes with that gorgeously blue and now sympathetic gaze. 'That's not a great way to start the day!'

She tried to smile but it was a wan effort and she abandoned it, making him frown. He leant slightly towards her, his eyes searching.

'Are you OK, Ellie?' he asked softly, and she shrugged.

'Of course. I'm just tired. And it could have been worse,' she said, forking up another mouthful of salad and trying not to think about the gorgeous eyes. 'At least none them had thrown up in the night or had a temperature, but I pity the people at nursery. Oscar was still screaming by the time we got there because I'd put him in the car without his shoes on, and Maisie was mutinous and grumpy for England.'

'And Evie? You did say Evie, didn't you?'

She felt her face soften into an involuntary smile at the thought of her baby girl and put her fork down, the salad forgotten. 'Yes, it's Evie. She was her usual sweet, sunny little self, bless her heart.'

He grinned, his eyes crinkling and making him suddenly even more approachable. 'Small mercies?' he murmured, and she laughed.

'Absolutely. I live for them, and I'm sure it won't be long before she gets the terrible twos and it all falls apart. I'm enjoying it while it lasts.'

He sat back, his eyes still searching hers thoughtfully. 'So, where's your husband while all this is going on?' he murmured.

The urge to smile evaporated, along with any trace of humour she'd been feeling, and she sat up straighter and dropped her eyes to her salad, prodding it around for something to do before she looked up again. 'No husband,' she said crisply. 'I'm divorced.'

'Ah. Join the club. I tell you what, let's not go there, shall we? It'll take all day and we've got much better things to discuss.'

It was his turn to look away, but not until she'd seen a subtle change in those fascinating eyes, a flicker of something like regret or disappointment or—grief? No matter. She was happy to let the subject drop and sip her coffee. Divorce was always a bit messy, and some were messier than others. Clearly not everything in life *had* gone his way...

'So, how long have you been working here?' he asked lightly, moving the subject on, and she was happy to pick it up and run with it.

'Since after Maisie, so a little over three years? We had a flat in London, but David's parents live in Yoxburgh and we'd bought a holiday home just round the corner from them, but he was away all the time working abroad so after we had Maisie we moved up here to our house and kept the flat on for when he was doing a fast turnaround, and I started work here when she was ten months old. And then two months in I realised I was pregnant with Oscar, which wasn't planned, and then Evie came along.'

Although she wasn't going into that, because David's reaction had devastated her. It still hurt now, nearly two years later, and probably always would, but she was fine without him. Better, really, no matter how tough it might be sometimes.

'So, how old are they now?' Nick asked softly.

'Maisie's just four, Oscar's two and a half, and Evie's nearly fifteen months.'

His eyes widened. 'That's...'

'Three in thirty-four months. I know. It's ridiculous.'

He let out a long, slow breath. 'I don't know about ridiculous, but that's pretty hardcore, for a single parent. For any parent, come to that, especially if you're working. It must be a nightmare.'

She shook her head. 'They're a joy, really, when I have time to draw breath and think about it. Today was just one of those days, but I wouldn't change it for the world, tantrums and all.'

'No, of course not. I'm sure you love them all dearly.'

'I do.' She eyed him steadily, wondering if she'd heard something odd in his voice. 'So, your turn. Why here?'

He shrugged. 'Why not? I wanted a total change, I don't have any ties, and it's the sort of job I've always wanted. I was ready for it, it was there—it seemed sort of meant.'

'What about your kids?' she asked, blatantly fishing, but he just shook his head, his eyes steady but expressionless now.

'No kids. If we'd had kids, I'd still be there.

Children are a lifetime commitment. You don't walk away. It's not negotiable.'

She gave a little snort. 'Tell it to the fairies. My ex walked out when I was eight weeks pregnant with Evie.'

He blinked, his eyes startled. 'Seriously? He left when you were pregnant? Did he know?'

He sounded appalled, and she couldn't help the bitter little laugh. Oh, yes, he'd known. It was why he'd gone.

'I thought we weren't going into this?' she said, trying to keep it light and move on, but he didn't let it drop.

'Does he see them?'

'Oh, yes. He comes up every fortnight and stays with his parents, who think it's dreadful that he walked out on his marriage, and they're not thrilled with me, either, because I won't have him back, but they're sticking by us because they want a decent relationship with their grandchildren, and the kids adore them. His loss.'

'And the children's. Idiot.' He held up a hand. 'Sorry, not my place.'

'Oh, no, feel free. Nobody's going to argue with you except him, and he's not here, thank goodness.' She gave him a wry smile. 'Just as well, or he'd be ranting at me for scraping my car on the wall this morning.'

He pulled a face, his mouth tipping ruefully up at one side. 'Sorry—again. I ought to pay for it to be fixed.'

'Why? You weren't driving it.'

'No, but it was my fault and I didn't exactly make your morning any better, did I? And I really am sorry about that. You obviously have enough on your plate.'

She answered his smile, wondering why that little tilt of his lips was having such a weird effect on her. Crazy—

'Yes, well, I think we need to forget all about it, and I think I need to do something a bit proactive or my afternoon's going to go down the tubes as well. I'm duty doctor this afternoon so I've got all sorts of patients slotted in. I need to go.'

She got to her feet, hesitated a second and then leant across the table, holding out her hand, telling herself it wasn't to find out if she felt that electric tingle again. 'Friends?' she asked, and he smiled and took her hand.

Yup, still there, fizzing all the way through her body.

'Friends,' he murmured, and she smiled and dropped his hand and straightened up, resisting the urge to rub her tingling palm on her trousers.

'Good. I'll see you on Monday, then,' she

said, as the door opened and Lucy Gallagher came in.

'You'll see him tonight at ours for dinner, I hope?' Lucy said, and she turned to her friend and colleague, her jaw dropping.

'Dinner?' she said blankly.

'Yes—Nick's welcome dinner?'

Oh, no. 'Isn't it next Friday?'

'No, it's tonight, at seven. Ah…' Lucy tilted her head to one side. 'No babysitter?'

She closed her eyes and counted to ten. Could Liz help out? Maybe. Another favour— oh, lord.

'No. I didn't need one, but David changed his weekend, and I didn't join the dots. Idiot me. I'm so, so sorry, Lucy. I'll ask my mother-in-law, and I'll let you know. I'll come if I possibly can, but it might just be for a short while.'

Lucy smiled and shook her head. 'Don't worry, I quite understand. Give her a ring, do what you can.'

'I will. I need to go; I've got a stack of patients. I'm sorry.'

She threw a vague smile in their direction, scooped up her coffee and headed for her room, her salad forgotten, but her hand was still tingling from his touch, scrambling her brain even further.

* * *

Liz said yes, bless her heart, and even volunteered to pick the children up from nursery for a sleepover, so after her surgery was finished she drove home, packed their things and dropped them round, then went back, threw the breakfast things in the dishwasher, brought in the washing off the line and then went to change. But into what?

She studied the contents of her wardrobe blankly, but nothing was right. Ridiculous. She was going for an informal supper with the rest of the doctors and their partners and the practice manager and her husband, just to welcome Nick. It didn't matter what she wore. Anything would do.

Except it wouldn't, somehow, because she'd already made a disastrous impression, and she wanted a chance to remedy that. If it wasn't already way too late…

So, the blue dress? No, too dressy. Pink? No. Too casual. Black? Too formal. OK, not a dress, then. Trousers and a top and pretty pumps?

Better—but which top?

She tried all of them, in the end, and went for the one that hung well, disguised her flabby bits and made her feel good about herself. That alone was quite an ask, but hey. Not that it mattered, she reminded herself crossly. The only thing that really mattered was getting there on time, because if she knew Lucy's husband, he would have been in the kitchen all day cooking up a storm, and the last thing she needed was to upset anyone else!

She touched up the makeup she'd hurled on hastily at six thirty this morning, slipped on her shoes and coat, grabbed the bottle of wine she'd bought for them and walked out without checking herself in the mirror again because it *just didn't matter*.

The Gallaghers only lived round the corner, and the drive would be full, so she walked, timing it so she'd be there just after seven so that hopefully some of the others would have arrived and she could melt into the background without having to talk to him. Not that she wanted to be rude to Nick, she'd done enough of that today to last a lifetime, but she didn't want to look over-keen either.

And heaven knows why she was letting it worry her! He was a work colleague, nothing more, and never would be. She'd be polite, friendly enough, and stop thinking about his cute behind and that lazy, oh-so-sexy smile. Surely she could manage that?

She arrived at five past seven, just as Dev and Reeta got there. Perfect.

Brian's car was there, and she could hear the others talking as Dev opened the door, but there was no sign of Nick's car on the drive. Had he walked? Or was he late? No. He didn't seem like the type to be late—or totally forget that he'd been invited for dinner.

Thank God for her mother-in-law. She would have been sunk without Liz in so many ways. The woman was a saint.

She plastered on a smile and followed Dev and Reeta in.

He was sitting in between Julia Wade, the practice manager, and Sarah Baines, another part-time doctor whose husband was at home with their children, and on the other side of Julia was Brian Rowlings, the practice principal. He'd met him and Julia before at his interviews, and also Dev Patel, the only other full-time doctor apart from him and Brian.

Dev was seated on the other side of the table, his wife Reeta, another part-time doctor, on one side and Ellie on his other, with Julia's husband next to Ellie on her other side, which put her right opposite him and gave him a perfect opportunity to study her. It was threatening to become a habit...

He dragged his eyes off her and looked up at their hosts. Lucy Gallagher, the most senior doctor after Brian, and her husband Andy, who he gathered was a part-time ED consultant at Yoxburgh Park Hospital, were busy piling food on dishes and setting them down along the length of the table, watched longingly by their black Labrador, Stanley.

'Just dig in, folks,' Andy said, so they did, passing things around, spoons waving in the air and not a trace of inhibition. It felt like a noisy, cheerful family Sunday lunch, he thought, not a formal introduction to the practice, and he liked it. He liked all of them, but he wanted to know more about them, most particularly Ellie.

He didn't get a chance to talk to her, though, because not surprisingly everyone wanted to ask him questions or tell him interesting and useful things about the practice, and he had to force himself to pay attention, but he was still aware of every breath she took.

After the main course they swapped places, and he ended up next to Ellie, which would have been fine if it hadn't been for the unmistakeable current of something seriously tempting that ran between them.

She wanted trifle but she couldn't reach it, so he stood up and leant across her, feeling the brush of her arm against his thigh as he picked it up, and he nearly dropped the dish.

'Here,' he said, sitting down again and holding it for her, then passing it across to Brian when she was done. And then Brian started to tell him things about the practice, things he probably needed to know, and at any other time would have been interested in, so he still didn't get to talk to her. Didn't mean he wasn't still utterly aware of her, of her scent, the sound of her laugh, the hitch in her breath and slight shift of her leg away from his as his thigh accidentally brushed hers—

'Coffee, anybody?' Lucy asked when they'd all ground to a halt, and Ellie shook her head.

'No, it's been lovely, Lucy, but I need to make a move. Sorry. I had a very early start and I'm running out of steam.'

'Yes, me, too,' he said, getting to his feet with a rueful smile. 'It's been great to meet you all, and I'm looking forward to working with you and getting to know you all much better, but I've got a lot to do over the weekend before I start on Monday. My house is in chaos and I need to be able to find my clothes, at the very least.'

'Give us a shout if you need a hand,' Andy offered, which produced a chorus of other offers, and he nodded and thanked them all, thanked Lucy and Andy for the meal and ended up on the drive at the same time as Ellie.

'Did you walk or are you driving?' he asked her.

'I walked—why?'

'So did I. I'll walk you home.'

'You don't need to do that—'

'Yes, I do. I don't want you on my conscience.'

She laughed at that. 'Nick, this is Yoxburgh! Nothing's going to happen to me.'

'Nevertheless,' he said with a smile, with no intention of backing down. 'And anyway, I want to talk to you. I have questions.'

She looked up at him, her face illuminated by the porch light, her expression sceptical as if she could see right through him. 'Such as?'

'Oh, practice stuff. Well, people stuff, really,' he added, improvising like crazy, but she nodded as if that seemed reasonable, and then turned away and set off, and he fell in beside her.

'So, ask away,' she prompted.

'Brian,' he said, because he genuinely was interested in what she had to say about him, so it seemed a good place to start.

She glanced at him. 'What about him?'

'He was on his own, and I understand he's

had some time off recently. Anything I should know?'

'Yes. His wife had early onset Alzheimer's, and he took time off and looked after her. She was only fifty-eight when she died last year, and she didn't know him for the last few months.'

He felt the weight of a familiar burden settle over him. 'That must have been difficult.'

'It was difficult. I covered what I could, but I was pregnant with Evie so we all picked up a bit and we got a locum for one day a week, and then she died and he came back a couple of months later. I think he was glad to get back to normal, to be honest. He'd been very isolated.'

He knew how that felt, when he'd been coping with his brother after Rachel had left him. He'd been hanging by a thread by the time Sam died. Still was, in a way.

'So, what else do you want to know?'

Nothing, really, but he drummed up a few questions to take his mind off Sam as much as anything, and then she came to a halt outside a surprisingly modest and fairly boring little eighties house—or at least it would have been, if it wasn't for the fact that it overlooked the sea.

'Well, this is me,' she said with a smile. 'See, no muggers or rapists or roving gangs.'

'No,' he said. 'Well, I'll say goodnight, then.'

She said nothing for a moment, and then looked up at him. 'Coffee?'

He tried to read her eyes, but it was too dark to see them properly. 'I thought you needed an early night?'

'I do, but I'm going to sit down first and chill for a while. It's been a hectic day. And we can talk more about the practice if you like. Up to you.'

The practice was the last thing on his mind. Getting to know her better, though...

'No, I don't fancy coffee.'

Did her face fall? Maybe, and he tipped his head on one side and smiled slowly. 'Tea, on the other hand...'

She let out a soft huff of laughter and turned away.

'You'd better come in, then.'

# CHAPTER TWO

It was a mess. Why had she invited him in? She must have been nuts.

'Come on through. I'm sorry, it's a bit of a tip. I left in a hurry this morning and I haven't had time to tidy it.'

He gave a quiet chuckle that did something weird to her nerve endings. 'Don't worry about it. I've seen much worse.'

'Very likely, but that doesn't mean I'm proud of it.'

He chuckled again, the sound soft and rich and oddly disturbing. She busied herself with the kettle, ridiculously aware of him behind her. What was he making of the house? And what did it matter what he thought of her *or* her house?

'Are these the kids' drawings?'

'Well, they're not mine,' she said with a laugh, turning back to him. He was studying the fridge, plastered with Oscar's little doodles and scrawlings, Maisie's almost recognisable pictures of a house and a bunch of flowers, and in the middle Evie's small messy handprints in pink and green and orange. He reached out a finger and traced a little handprint, and there was a wistful smile on his face that touched her heart.

*Why doesn't he have children?*

'How do you take your tea?'

He turned back to her, the smile becoming suddenly more generic as he hid whatever feelings they'd been that she'd had that little glimpse of. 'Oh, white, no sugar, as it comes.' He glanced around, frowning slightly. 'So how do you get to the garden? I take it there is a garden?'

'Oh, yes, it's a nice garden once you get to it, but you have to go through the sitting room—or out of the front and round the side.'

His eyebrow twitched. 'That's handy for the bin.'

She laughed again, this time with real irony. 'You don't say. The layout's ridiculous. Someone blocked up the kitchen door that led to the garden, and yes, it's handy to have more cupboard and worktop space, but a back door would be handy, too. If you can stand the mess, I'll give you a guided tour while the kettle boils.'

He chuckled again. 'I can stand the mess,' he said, and followed her, eyeing the house curiously as she pointed out the interesting features, like where the back door should have been, the lack of a utility room, the dining room with the wasted sea view, the three cramped bedrooms and tiny bathroom.

'It's not what I expected.'

'What did you expect? Pristine tidiness?'

He laughed and looked down at her, his eyes gentle. 'No, I didn't mean that at all. This is just normal family mess. I wasn't expecting a sea view. You were lucky to get it. They're always at a premium.'

'Absolutely. That's why we bought it. David never did anything by accident—well, not a lot,' she added economically, and headed down the stairs. 'And the sea view would be fine if I ever had time to look at it, but even if I did, you can hardly see it because of the stupid layout. The house isn't big enough for three children, but I can't afford to extend it or move house, and David's attitude is if I want to do things to it, or move to something better, then all I have to do is have him back.'

'I take it that's not an option,' he ventured cautiously.

She laughed at that, a brittle little tinkle of sound, and led him back to the kitchen. 'I don't think it's a serious suggestion anyway, so even if I thought it was a good idea, which I definitely don't, I'm still stuck here.'

'So what were you planning to do?'

'Move the sitting room to the front and the dining room to the back because it's as far from the kitchen as you can get at the moment, and extend it out into the garden to make a family area and put another bedroom and bathroom on. That way at least there would be a sea view from a room that would be used, rather than just the dining room, which I hardly use, and my bedroom, where I sleep with the curtains shut. As I said, wasted.'

'That's not wasted! You could lie in bed with a cup of tea in the mornings and look at the sea. Bliss.'

'With three small children crawling all over me? That's not bliss, that's asking for trouble.'

His face softened into a wry grin. 'Yeah, maybe. But the downstairs layout is crazy, I'll give you that. I'd probably just open it all up if you didn't want to spend a lot.'

'But then there'd be nowhere where I could just retreat and know it's going to be tidy and not covered in toys. Here, your tea,' she said, handing it to him, and led him back into the sitting room, sweeping little wooden blocks out of the way with her feet, and behind him she heard that chuckle again.

'You need a fairy, Ellie. Someone to come in while everyone's sleeping and tidy it all up.'

She rolled her eyes and curled up on the sofa. 'Er—that would be me? Nice idea, though. I wonder if the tooth fairy has a cousin who's looking for work?' she added with a grin, and he gave a soft huff of laughter and sat down opposite her, stretching his legs out with that little wince she'd noticed earlier.

'Are you OK?' she asked, and he tilted his head slightly.

'OK?'

'You winced.'

'Oh, that. No, it's an old fracture. It plays up a bit if I've overdone it. It's nothing.'

'Overdone it? You sat in the staff room or the office for a lot of the day, and you've been sitting down at dinner.'

'That's today. Yesterday I moved all my stuff up here into my new house. There was a lot of lifting and lugging.'

'Didn't you have a removal company?'

He smiled. 'Yes. There's still a lot of lugging around to be done. My fault. I should have been more specific about where I wanted things. Anyway, it's all in the right place now, more or less. All I have to do is unpack.'

She wondered where the house was, but it seemed rude to ask—except he'd seen every inch of her chaotic and overcrowded little house, so the location of his could hardly be a state secret. Even if it was none of her business...

'Where is it?' she asked, finally giving in to her curiosity.

'Just round the corner, on a little private road with half a dozen or so houses on it near the steps to the beach.'

'Jacob's Lane. Wow. I know it well. There are some lovely houses there. Which one is it?' she asked, totally forgetting that she wasn't supposed to be being nosy.

'Split-level timber thing on the right, built in the seventies, with a weird mono-pitch roof?'

'I know the one, it's been empty for a while. I really like it.'

'Yeah, me, too. It's nothing from the front but it's quite interesting inside, and it's got a lovely courtyard style walled garden—and all the rooms open onto it. The only thing lacking is the sea view, but I've got legs and it's hardly far away.'

That quirky grin again, which seemed to have some magic power over her.

Why? Why him, her new colleague? Although he seemed to have forgiven her for her tirade this morning, so she should be grateful for that, and she could live with a bit of unrequited lust in the interests of a peaceful and amicable working relationship.

'So does it need a lot of work?'

'Not really. Just an injection of my taste and a bit of tweaking.'

'Not a project like this was meant to be, then?'

He gave a soft laugh and shook his head. 'No. I didn't want that, not now, not at this point in my life. I've had enough challenges. I'm ready for a quiet life.'

She chuckled softly. 'Me, too, but there's not much chance of that with three small people. Frankly I'd settle for six hours' sleep a night. That would help.'

Just the thought made her want to cry with longing, and she was running out of steam. She stifled a little yawn, and apologised, but he gave her a wry smile.

'I need to go. You've had a long day and I'm keeping you up, so I'll leave you to what's left of that early night you wanted. Maybe you'll get more than six hours.'

'Oh, bliss. I might even take a cup of tea up in the morning and look at my sea view. That would be a novelty.'

He chuckled and got to his feet—that wince,

again—and headed into the kitchen with his mug, setting it down on the worktop before he walked to the front door. Then he turned and smiled down at her, his eyes gentle, and her stomach flipped over.

'Thanks for the tea and the guided tour, and for filling me in on the practice.'

'You're welcome. Thank you for walking me home, even if it wasn't strictly necessary. I'll see you on Monday.'

'I'll look forward to it.'

He hesitated for a moment, then cupped her shoulders in his hands and touched a kiss to her cheek, then dropped his hands, turned away and headed off in the direction of his house.

She watched him go from the open doorway, her fingers tracing the tingle on her cheek. She'd felt the slight graze of stubble on her skin as he'd kissed her, breathed in the scent of his skin against hers, and her breath caught.

Crazy. Her mind was scrambled by a mixture of tiredness, the two glasses of wine she'd had with dinner, and her unexpected reaction to a man she'd been convinced she'd dislike.

And she didn't dislike him at all, she realised. She liked him. Liked him a lot, and wanted to know more—such as why he didn't have children, why his marriage had gone wrong, and why he'd moved here on what seemed like a whim. For the quiet life he'd talked about?

Too many questions, and none of those things were anything to do with her. Just a colleague. Nothing more.

'Get a grip, Ellie,' she told herself, and closed the door firmly.

Damn.

Why was she so nice?

Stupid, really, but he hadn't wanted her to be. Not a woman with three children. A woman with three children definitely wasn't on his agenda, and there was no way on earth he was going there.

So what was with the pang of regret?

He missed his footing slightly in the dark, and his ankle wrenched a little, taking his mind off her.

Not before time. They had to work together, and the last thing he needed in a new job that he hoped would be a long-term, settled future for him was an inappropriate reaction to an inappropriate woman.

He crunched over the gravel drive, slid his key into the lock and closed the front door behind him with a sigh. Boxes everywhere, stacked up in every room. Boxes containing his life—and some of Samuel's. Not that he was ready to unpack those yet. Might never be.

Navigating his way to the kitchen, he put the kettle on, made himself a cup of chamomile tea and turned up the heating. Not that it was particularly cold, but the house had been empty for months, and it needed warmth and life injected back into it.

A fridge smothered in multicoloured handprints and colourful scrawls? Blocks and cars and jigsaw pieces all over the floor?

Hardly. He'd leave that to Ellie.

Not that he had a choice. His own stupidity had taken care of that, but at least his sisters had provided their parents with grandchildren, so that box was ticked. One small thing that he didn't have to feel guilty about.

He went up the few steps to the sitting room, dropped onto the sofa, went to reach for the TV remote and changed his mind. Instead he leant back with a sigh, cradling his tea and letting his mind run back over the evening and all he'd learnt.

Brian was a widower, working part-time but for how long Ellie didn't seem to know, and as for the others, they were a cheerful, friendly bunch of people he'd be happy to work with. It would be nice to be part of a team again, after four years of patchy locum work as his brother had grown steadily more dependent. He'd taken time out to help his parents, but he'd missed it, missed the camaraderie, the belonging.

He wanted to belong again, and from what he'd seen so far, he'd be welcomed with open arms by the other practice members.

And then there was Ellie.

Ellie, with her long dark hair, grey-green eyes that showed every emotion, and that wickedly dry sense of humour. Not to mention a curvy, womanly body that made him ache to wrap her up in his arms and kiss her senseless.

No, that would be him who'd be senseless, because it wasn't just her eyes and her wit and her lush, beautiful body. It was her three very small children, all part of the same package, and he wanted nothing to do with it.

*Liar.*

He sighed again, sipped the chamomile tea and pulled a face. The tea was the last thing he wanted, but he had no idea where he'd put the bottle of single malt he kept for the times when he wanted to drown his sorrows and wallow in self-pity, and maybe that was just as well.

He had a lot to do tomorrow, and he needed

to spend Sunday resting or his hip and ankle were going to give him hell.

He got to his feet, went back down to the kitchen, poured the tea down the sink and went to bed.

Just because the damage was already done, the children were saints on Monday morning, and she dropped them off at nursery and walked into the practice at ten past eight with plenty of time to prepare for her morning surgery.

She'd vowed not to drive so that Nick could have the parking space, this time without argument, and there was no sign of his car as she arrived. How gratifying—

'Morning!'

He appeared at the top of the stairs as she put her foot on the bottom step, and she couldn't help the wry smile.

'Your car isn't here. I thought I'd beaten you to it.'

His mouth kicked up, and she felt a strange sensation in her chest, a weird flutter that brought a tiny glow with it. What *was* it about that smile that it seemed to light up the corners of her heart?

'Sorry to disappoint. I've been here since half seven. Lucy and Julia came in early so they could talk me through my day. It's looking busy already.'

'It will be. It's always busy. Have you had a cup of tea?'

'No, I've had coffee, but the kettle's hot. I'll be up again in a minute.'

She nodded and headed up, passing him on the stairs. Wasn't that supposed to be unlucky? Except that the stairs were wide and she'd hardly felt the brush of his arm against hers.

Even so, it had left a little tingle in its wake—or was that the fresh scent of soap or shower gel that lingered in the air? She recognised it from Friday, when they'd been seated side by side at Andy and Lucy's table, and again when he'd kissed her as he'd left. Not aftershave or cologne, more subtle than that, but it had made her want to rest her head against his chest and breathe him in—

*Pull yourself together! You've got work to do. Enough of the daydreaming and fantasy. He's just a colleague.*

And if she told herself that often enough, maybe it'd sink in. She made a cup of tea, took it down to her consulting room and logged into her computer, and there was a tap on the door.

'Come in!'

It was Nick, sticking his head round the

door with a serious look on his face. 'Have you got two minutes? One of your patients is down to see me and he'd rather see you, apparently, only your list is full. James Golding?'

'Oh, Jim. Yes, of course I can see him. He's a dear old boy and he never makes a fuss. He's had a triple bypass but he still gets angina from time to time, so it might be that. I'll get Katie to swap it over.'

'OK. I think he might be here already, actually.'

'Sounds likely. I'll see him now. You could take my first patient, if you like. I have no idea who they are so there's no continuity of care issue.'

'Done. I'll see Katie. Thanks.'

'Don't thank me. I'd rather see Mr Golding myself because there must be something going on. He doesn't like to make a fuss, so I'll check him over thoroughly.'

'Good. Thanks. See you later, maybe.'

They shared a smile, and she went out into the waiting room and spotted Jim Golding, tucked into the corner with his hands knotted round the handle of his walking stick. She went over and perched beside him.

'Morning, Jim. I gather you wanted to see me?' she murmured, and he looked up and gave her a weary smile.

'They said you were busy,' he said, his voice distressed.

'No. We've swapped. You're with me. Do you want to come now?'

Not that she really had time, because there was always a ton of admin to do before she could start and it was going to put her behind, but there was something about the cautious way he stood up that set alarm bells ringing.

'No rush,' she said gently, and ushered the frail, elderly man into her consulting room and settled him in the chair. 'So, Jim, tell me what's going on.'

'How was he?'

Ellie put her cup down with a plonk next to the kettle, not sure where to start, and he got up and went over to her.

'Ellie? What's up?'

She pulled a face. 'I'm not sure. He said he was OK but he'd had a twinge or two, so I've sent him to see Megan for a twelve-lead ECG and a raft of bloods. Just to be on the safe side. He also wanted me to draw up a DNAR.'

'Really?'

She nodded. 'Yes, and I don't like it. I think there's something going on that he hasn't told me. Gut instinct?'

He gave a soft huff of laughter. 'Yeah, I know the feeling. Sometimes I hate my gut.'

'Don't hate it. Trust it. I trust mine and it's giving me grief right now.'

His mouth kicked up into a fleeting smile. 'You could be being overcautious.'

Or not, as it turned out, because when she was back in her consulting room wading through test results, she heard a yell and went out to find Nick on his knees in the corridor, bent over Mr Golding.

'What's happened?'

'I don't know. An MI, maybe? We need to move him and repeat the ECG. Oh, hang on. No, no, no, no, don't do this!'

She turned back to find Nick had the elderly man's shirt open and was listening to his chest.

'Anything?'

He shook his head and started doing chest compressions. 'No. He's arrested. Can you call an ambulance?'

'No. Nick, stop.' She dropped to her knees beside him and covered his hands with her own, stilling them. 'He's got a DNAR, remember? He signed it before he went in with Megan. We can't resuscitate him and I wouldn't want to. His wife died last year, he's really struggled without her. He doesn't want this.'

'Is it in his notes?'

'Yes. I put it on the computer, and we have the physical document on file. He signed it in front of witnesses.'

His hands slowly lifted, and he stared down at the man for a long moment before he shut his eyes and sat back on his heels.

'We need to close off the corridor and move him somewhere until they get here to take him away. I'll do that, you call the office and get an ambulance.'

She nodded, went back into her surgery and asked Katie to call an ambulance, and then left a message on Jim's daughter's voicemail asking her to call. She ought to call in her next patient, there was no time to grieve for the patient she'd grown very fond of over the past few months, but somehow her heart was heavy and she just needed a moment…

Something splashed on her hand and she swiped it away, and then she heard her door open and she turned, as Nick's arms closed around her.

'I'm sorry I couldn't save him,' he murmured, the sound echoing through his chest under her ear.

She shook her head and eased away a little, feeling suddenly awkward. 'Don't be. It's what he wanted. I just wish I could have done more to help him.'

He let go of her, one hand coming up to wipe a tear gently from her cheek. 'You helped him get what he wanted in the end, Ellie. He went very quickly, and he wasn't distressed. I think he knew what was happening.'

She nodded, hauled in a breath and straightened up, blew her nose and tried to smile. 'We aren't supposed to get involved.'

'No. We're not.' But his smile said it all, and with a quick check to make sure she was really OK, he went back to his patients and left her to deal with Mr Golding's daughter.

'I'm sorry you lost a patient on your first day. Are you OK?'

He looked up into Ellie's concerned eyes, closed the file he was working on, shut the lid of his laptop and stood up. 'I'm fine, Ellie. It happens, people reach the end of the road, and anyway he wasn't my patient. How about you? Are you OK?'

'Yes, I'm fine,' she said, but he wasn't convinced.

'You're working late tonight.'

She shook her head. 'No. I always do an evening surgery on Mondays. It's a busy day but I'm done now. I'm glad I caught you, though.

I spoke to Mr Golding's daughter and broke the news, and she rang back later after she'd been to see him to thank us for looking after him and for letting him go when we did. Apparently he'd rung her and said I was making him have all sorts of silly tests, but I'd been really kind so he was indulging me.'

'Do you know what he said to me, when I found him on the floor? "Oh, dear, I'm making such a fuss."'

She swallowed, as if she had a lump in her throat, and let out a soft laugh—to diffuse her emotions, maybe?

'That's so typical. He was such a gentleman,' she murmured, and her wistful smile warmed something deep inside him and made him want to hold her again, because frankly that tiny hug this morning for a sad colleague had been nothing like enough.

'Do you have to collect the children?'

'No. Liz takes them back to mine and gets them ready for bed.'

'I'll walk you home then. I'm done now.'

She hesitated, then nodded and gave him a weary smile.

'OK. But just to the end of your road. I'll walk the rest of the way on my own.'

'Because you don't want your mother-in-law getting ideas?'

She laughed, probably because he'd hit the nail right on the head. 'Something like that. And anyway, you don't need to be exposed to the monsters at the end of the day. They can be pretty grim when they're tired.'

He smiled and shook his head, not in the least concerned about the children, or the mother-in-law, come to that. And anyway, he had to get home.

'Don't worry about it. I need to get back to the dog anyway.'

'Dog?' Her eyes widened in surprise. 'I didn't know you had a dog. You said you didn't have any commitments.'

His smile felt a little off kilter. 'I didn't, not until yesterday when my parents delivered him. He's my brother's dog.'

'Your brother's? So how come you've got him?'

He looked away so she couldn't read his eyes. 'He died last year,' he said economically, and felt the usual sick feeling in the pit of his stomach.

'Oh, Nick, I'm so sorry. I had no idea.'

Her voice was filled with compassion and it choked him for a moment so he picked up his bag and slung it over his shoulder as they headed down the stairs.

'No reason why you should have known,'

he said. 'Anyway, Rufus kind of adopted me while it was all going on, and he's been pining for me since I left last week, apparently, so I said I'd have him. They've been in Kettering with my sister, so they just popped over for the afternoon and dropped him off.'

He held the door for her, and then fell into step beside her.

'So what is Rufus?' she asked.

'Cavalier King Charles spaniel. He's a nice little thing, and very placid. He spent most of his life on Samuel's bed, and he used to let us know when he was about to have a seizure, which was totally unexpected and incredibly useful.'

'Was he a trained seizure alert dog, then?'

He shook his head. 'No. He had no training at all, and he was chronically disobedient, but he just latched onto Sam and he was amazing with him. He really calmed him, and even when Sam didn't recognise us any more he knew Rufus.'

'Poor dog. He must have been gutted when your brother died.'

He swallowed and drew in a long breath. 'Yeah,' he said, and left it at that, mainly because he couldn't say any more. How could it still feel so raw, over a year later?

'What had happened to him? To Samuel?'

He shrugged. 'He was born with very complex needs. Nobody could say why, but he was very compromised in all sorts of ways, and my parents' lives revolved around him for thirty-eight years.' And not just their lives. His, too, but that was another matter.

And there was that lump in his throat again, which didn't get any better when she rested her hand lightly on his arm.

'I'm so sorry.'

He nodded, and kept walking, and then they were at the end of his road and he slowed to a halt and smiled at her.

'Right, this is me. I take it you can find the way from here?'

She rolled her eyes at him, then cocked her head on one side and studied him thoughtfully. 'Are you OK?'

'Yes, of course I am. Why shouldn't I be?'

Her smile was tender and nearly pushed him over the edge. 'Because you're sad?'

He was. Sad, and guilty, because there'd been an element of relief when Sam had finally slipped away and he'd been free of the burden, and he was filled with shame about that.

He found a smile and pinned it on. 'I'm fine, Ellie. Will I see you tomorrow?'

She nodded. 'I work Monday, Tuesday and Friday.'

'I'll have the kettle on for you,' he promised, and her mouth curved into a grin, and she went up on tiptoe and brushed a kiss on his cheek.

'You do that. Take care, Nick. I'll see you tomorrow,' she murmured, and turned and walked away, leaving him feeling oddly— lonely? He watched her till she was out of sight, and then let himself into his house and went to find Rufus.

He wasn't hard to find. The little dog was curled up in his bed in the hall beside the boxes of Samuel's possessions, and he lifted his head and wagged his tail in greeting, his eyes huge and sad as ever.

'Hi, little guy,' he said gently, his voice gruff and scratchy, and as he crouched down Rufus got to his feet, put his paws on his chest, whined softly and licked his face.

'I'm sorry, mate. I'm a pretty poor substitute, aren't I?' he murmured gruffly, but Rufus wagged his tail and sat down, looking hopeful.

He gave the little dog another stroke, straightened up and went into the kitchen, hauling in a long breath. 'Come on, then, little man. Let's find some supper, and then you need a walk, and we'll see if we can find

something nice on the telly later, shall we?'
he murmured, and Rufus followed him, tail
wafting gently, his mournful eyes fixed on
Nick's every move.

# CHAPTER THREE

SHE HARDLY SAW Nick the next day, but as promised the kettle had just boiled when she got in, which made her smile. They passed on the stairs, and she asked him fleetingly if he was OK.

'Of course I am. Why wouldn't I be?' he asked.

But she wasn't bringing his brother up again, especially not at work, so she just smiled and said, 'Good,' and moved on.

She saw him later at the other end of the corridor outside the consulting rooms and he flashed her a smile, but that was all they had time for and she left at the end of the day without seeing him again.

Oddly, though, just knowing he was in the building made her feel different about it, that little tingle of anticipation that if she turned the corner he might be there. Which was ridiculous, because he was *just a colleague*. If she told herself that often enough, maybe it would sink in.

She spent Wednesday with the children, playing in the garden, and on Thursday they wanted to go the beach with buckets and spades. She'd been trying not to think about Nick, except of course they walked past his house on the way and she couldn't help but study it and think about him.

She'd love to see inside it, but it probably wasn't a good idea, not the way she reacted to him. She chivvied the children past it, but then it started to rain as they got to the top of the steps so they ran back and she took them to a soft play centre instead and spent the time lecturing herself for being so obsessed by him.

It was still raining on Friday morning, but it didn't matter as she had the car with her. She'd dropped the children's things off at Liz and Steven's on the way to the nursery because it was David's rescheduled weekend with them, and as she turned into the car park she crossed her fingers that Nick hadn't driven, too.

He hadn't, or at least he hadn't arrived yet, which seemed unlikely. He'd always been there before her even when she'd made good time, and today of course she'd been on the drag again after another emotional meltdown from Oscar over the missing shoe, which still hadn't turned up.

Still, summer was coming, and she'd buy him some sandals next week.

She went up to the staff room, and the kettle was still fairly hot, but there was no sign of him and she felt a strange sense of anti-climax. Stupid. She made a coffee, headed downstairs and waded through a pile of prescription requests and results before seeing her first patient, and she didn't see Nick until after she'd finished her lunch.

'Are you hiding from me?' she asked jokingly as they passed on the stairs, and he stopped and grinned.

'Now, why would I do that? Actually I've been hoping to see you. Am I right in thinking you're child-free this weekend?'

She nodded, puzzled that he should ask. 'Why?'

'I just wondered if you'd like to be my first guest? If you haven't got anything better to do, that is, which you probably have.'

She felt a smile edging in, and tried to moderate it so she didn't look too ridiculously keen. 'Well, now, let me see. There's sorting the washing, or cleaning the house from top to bottom, or weeding the garden...'

'Is that a no?'

'Absolutely not,' she told him, letting the smile out. 'When were you thinking?'

'I don't know. Whenever you like. Dinner tonight, or tomorrow, or lunch tomorrow, or Sunday—whatever. I'm easy.'

She mentally scanned her fridge and came up with not a lot, or nothing that wouldn't keep. 'Tonight would be nice, but that's a bit short notice for you, isn't it, unless you're planning on getting a takeaway?'

He shook his head. 'I've got an internet order coming at seven. Tonight would be fine.'

'Can you cook?'

He chuckled. 'What if I say no?'

'I'll eat first,' she said, unable to stop the little laugh, and he joined in, shaking his head again slowly, that lazy, sexy smile doing strange things to her pulse.

'You don't need to eat first. I can cook. Any special dietary requirements?'

She shook her head, and he grinned.

'Well, that's a relief, since I've already done the order. So—seven thirty?'

She felt a little bubble of excitement burst in her chest. 'Seven thirty sounds fine. Can I bring anything?'

'No. I have everything covered. Just bring yourself and an appetite.'

He felt nervous.

Why, for heaven's sake? It wasn't as if it was a date, not in that sense. He'd just invited a colleague around for a meal, a sort of impromptu housewarming, and he wasn't going to do anything elaborate.

The entrance hall doubled as a dining room, so the first thing he had to do was find the table under the pile of boxes he'd dumped on it, so he shifted them into one of the bedrooms, hesitated over the pile of Sam's boxes on the floor and then moved them, too. It might worry Rufus, but he dug out Sam's old blanket and put it in his bed, tucked in the corner under the stairs. Maybe that would be enough.

Right. The table was clear, the floor was clear bar the dog bed, the kitchen was clean anyway because he'd been using it for a week, and the moment the delivery came he turned on the oven and started to prep the salmon parcels.

By the time Ellie arrived the fish was ready to go in the oven, he'd made the avocado and sweet chilli salad starter, the rice was cooked, the melting middle chocolate puddings, his one concession to laziness, were unwrapped and ready to go, and the wine was nicely chilled.

He heard the crunch of gravel and opened the door as she stepped onto the porch, a pot plant in her hand and a smile on her face, and he felt an odd sensation in his chest.

'Here. A little housewarming present,' she said, and he took it with a smile, kissed her cheek and ushered her in, trying to ignore the weird thing going on with his heart.

By the time he'd put the plant down she was on the floor, making a fuss of Rufus, who was rolling on his back for a tummy-rub.

'Oh, he's really sweet,' she murmured, smiling tenderly at the shameless little flirt, and he chuckled.

'He is. He's a nice little dog, and he'll stand any amount of that, but he's normally quite shy, probably because he's had a sheltered life.'

'Well, he doesn't seem shy now,' Ellie said with a laugh, getting to her feet, and then she looked around curiously, glancing up the short flight of stairs on her left.

'So what's up there?'

'The sitting room. Let's get a drink and take it up there. It overlooks the garden and it's still light, so you'll be able to see it—unless you want a guided tour first?'

She laughed, the sound rippling through him and reactivating that heart nonsense, and her eyes were twinkling.

'Absolutely. I'm insanely curious. I've walked past this house so many times on our way to the beach, and I've always wanted to know what it was like inside because it's so unusual and it fascinates me. Can we?'

'Sure. We can take our drinks with us. It won't take long to look at it and it'll probably be a dreadful anti-climax.' He headed into the kitchen and glanced back at her. 'Are you OK with white wine or do you want something else?'

'White's fine. Thanks. Wow, it's a good-sized kitchen.'

'Good-sized everything, really. The bedrooms aren't huge, but they're big enough and there are four of them, so if either of my sisters wants a seaside holiday I can accommodate them and their families, so it sort of makes sense even though it's just me. Come and see. We'll do the bedroom wing first, then go up to the sitting room.'

'Wing? That sounds very grand.'

He chuckled. 'No. It's not grand at all, it's pretty basic, really. Very simple, but that suits me. I'm a simple man.'

There was nothing simple about him, she thought as she followed him. A single man who had no ties and responsibilities, buying a family-sized house so his sisters could come for a seaside holiday with their children? A dog who'd belonged to his late brother and had been pining for him, so he'd adopted it? And yet he'd left them all to move to Yoxburgh. Why?

He led her through a little dogleg and down the narrow hall that ran away from the front of the house, opening doors and gesturing as he went.

'So the bedrooms are on this side, all overlooking the garden, and the service rooms like the bathrooms and utility room are across the corridor because they don't need a view. It's not fancy but it seems to work.'

'I'm sure it does,' she said, peering into the first bedroom. It was long and narrow, with a window at the far end, but she couldn't see a lot more than that. 'You've got a lot of boxes.' Surely more than one man could need in a lifetime.

He glanced at them and nodded. 'Yes. I have. My life's been in boxes since Rachel left and we sold the house.'

'Rachel's your wife, I assume?'

'My ex-wife. Yes. She—uh—she walked.'

Like David...

'So, anyway, some of the boxes are from that, and my parents packed up all Samuel's stuff and had no idea what to do with it, so I've got all that here, too. Heaven knows what I'll do with it all, but it seemed wrong to throw his life away and I'm not short of space. I guess I'll sort it sometime.'

She turned to look at him keenly, concerned, and he looked away as if he didn't want her reading him.

'You think about him a lot, don't you?' she said softly, and he gave a little huff of laughter but didn't answer, just led her back out of the room and down the corridor, pushing the doors open so she could see the other rooms. The next two were the same as the first, and then he pushed open the last door and stood back.

'This is mine. It's bigger than the others, obviously, and it's got a dressing room and en suite, and a door to the garden, which is nice.'

She looked around, taking in the space, the simple lines of the furniture, the bed made up with crisp white linen without a single mucky handprint on it, and sighed. 'Oh, I'm so jealous of all your space,' she said with a wry laugh, and turned back to him, catching a glimpse of something curiously like guilt.

Why on earth would he feel guilty?

'Seen enough?' he asked, and turned and walked away anyway, because he'd suddenly seen it with her eyes and he wished he'd never shown it to her, because although it was never going to be anything that special, this house would be ideal for her and her children, unlike the one she'd got, for which she'd had had such grand plans until her husband had walked.

He wondered why, but it didn't seem right to ask and he didn't want to bring it up because once they started on that conversation there was a world of stuff on his side that she might want to know, and he really, really didn't want to talk about it.

'Come on, let's go and put the fish in the oven—are you OK with teriyaki salmon parcels and rice?'

'Oh, no, it sounds awful,' she said, but her eyes were giving her away so he stifled a laugh and went back to the kitchen and put the fish in the oven, then topped up their glasses and led her up to the sitting room.

'Oh, this is a lovely room! I love the sloping ceiling—it brings in so much light! And what a fabulous sunset! Look at it!'

'I know. I could sit and watch the sky changing all day long.' He lifted down a dish of nuts and raisins from the bookcase, and offered it to her. 'Just keep Rufus out of them because of the raisins.'

'Would he steal food?'

He looked down at Rufus, sitting at her feet and begging shamelessly, and laughed.

'What do you think?'

The food was wonderful. Simple, fresh, perfectly cooked and utterly delicious.

Rather like her host. Well, not simple. There was nothing simple about Nick Cooper, as she'd already thought, but now, after spending the last hour or so with him, lingering over their dinner, she'd seen more of that other side of him. There was a whole world of stuff going on behind his eyes, and she had no idea who or what had hurt him most, but he'd certainly been affected badly by his brother's death.

Survivor guilt? Maybe. Or maybe just plain grief.

They were back in the sitting room, with her curled up in the corner of a sofa, him sprawled on an adjacent one at right angles and a box of after-dinner mints between them, and she turned her head and searched his eyes in the lamp light.

'Tell me about your brother,' she said softly.

He looked away, his body utterly still, and she wished she hadn't asked, but it was too late now and maybe he needed to talk.

'What do you want to know?'

'Not the medical stuff. The other stuff.

What was he like, what could he do, what was your role?'

He met her eyes again. 'My role?'

She nodded, searching his eyes, but they weren't giving anything away. 'Every family with a disabled child has altered priorities. It's inevitable. I guess you found that.'

He held her eyes, and for a fleeting second the shutters opened and she saw raw pain and regret, then he looked away again.

'Yeah, I guess you could say that. So, my role.' He shrugged. 'I was his brother. You know the song "He Ain't Heavy, He's My Brother"? It's not that simple. He was a lead weight in my life, but he was also an anchor, someone to listen, someone who loved me unconditionally.'

'Could he communicate?'

'Oh, yes. He could talk, sort of. I could understand him, and we used to have fun before he got too ill. It was OK when we were kids, it was just normal for me, what life was, but then when I was twelve and he was eleven, my mother got accidentally pregnant with twins. And everything changed.'

'Everything?'

He nodded. 'My father gave up his job and started working from home, so he could be there to support my mother, and more and more of Samuel's care fell on me. Obviously I was going to school and so was he, when he was well enough. He went to a special school and they'd come and pick him up in their adapted minibus, but in the evenings and at weekends and in the holidays, more and more it was me hanging out with him so Mum could be with the girls and Dad could work. And we stopped going out, really, because Samuel was getting heavier and it was harder to move four kids with the wheelchair, too, and it was a special chair, a bit reclined, so getting a vehicle that would take us all was impossibly hard. I think it just got too difficult, to be honest, so we stopped doing it.'

'So your family life revolved around your home and your brother?'

He nodded. 'Yes. Totally. And because my father needed to earn a living it ended up with me being asked to look after the girls or Samuel, so Mum could do the other stuff. I was nearly seventeen by then, wanted my own life, and the girls were five and wanted to do things I hated, so I was spending my life either shut in a room with Sam while I did my homework or revision, or hanging out in playgrounds and supervising the girls in the garden and trying to keep them out of trouble, and all I got from them was, "You're not our daddy, you can't tell us what to do." So I decided it was my turn.'

She frowned at that, because there was something in his voice that made her blood run cold. 'Your turn?'

He swallowed. 'Yeah. For some reason I thought it would be a good idea to ride my bike off the garage roof.'

She felt her eyes widen. 'What? How? Why?'

His chuckle held a world of pain. 'To get attention? I knew I'd hurt myself, but I was past caring. It was the summer holidays, I was sick of being used, and our garden was on a slope, with the garage cut into the bank. It stuck up about three feet at the back, so I found a plank, propped it up against the back wall to make a ramp, rode my bike down the hill, up the plank, straight across the garage roof and onto the drive.' He gave her a slightly twisted little grin and put another mint chocolate in his mouth. 'Needless to say it didn't end well.'

She felt sick. 'What happened?'

'My left pedal broke as I landed, so I trashed my ankle, crashed down onto the crossbar and shattered my pelvis.' He paused for a moment, then added with a wry smile, 'There was a bit of other collateral damage in the area, too.'

Her eyes widened. 'Collateral damage?'

His smile was wry and hid a world of pain.

'Let's just say that's why Rachel and I never had children—well, one of the reasons.'

Good grief. She could only imagine what he might have done, and none of it was good. 'Did you pass out?'

He laughed again, that hollow chuckle she was getting used to, and shook his head. 'Sadly not, not for a single second. Well, not until the paramedics arrived and straightened out my ankle. That wasn't fun. None of it was fun, to be fair, and my parents were distraught, my sisters were in floods of tears, I could hear Samuel calling because he'd realised something was going on, and I just felt sick. That could have been pain, of course, but whatever. I had their attention, at least.'

'And did it help you?'

That laugh again. 'No. No, of course not, not in any way. Well, it did, eventually, I suppose. I realised a little better what Samuel went through on a daily basis if nothing else. There's nothing like being a teenage boy and having someone else wipe your—well, whatever, independence with personal care is something I now prize very highly.'

'I bet you do. Poor you.'

'Poor me? I was an idiot. It was a stupid thing to do, and I got exactly what I deserved. My parents, though, didn't deserve any of it, and all it did was stress and upset them even more, so on top of the resentment was a whole world of guilt. I pulled myself together after that, once I got out of hospital, and so did they a bit, in that they'd ask me how I felt about doing things to help out, and I learned to tell them. It was a revelation for all of us.'

She frowned at that. 'I don't understand.'

'I'd never complained. Anything they asked me to do, I just did it, and the resentment got bigger and bigger until I couldn't cope with it.'

'Hence the crazy stunt?'

'Hence the crazy stunt. My father called me an idiot, and he was absolutely spot-on. I'll live with the consequences of it for ever. That's what happens with self-inflicted life-changing injuries. You get the rest of your life to remind yourself you were an idiot—and if that comes over as self-pitying, it's not meant to. I know it was my fault, I've accepted that, and I've come to terms with the consequences and learned to live with it.'

She wasn't convinced. 'How long were you in hospital? You must have had some horrendous damage,' she said contemplating the extensive microsurgery he must have had.

'Weeks. I don't know how many. I missed the start of the autumn term, I know that. Plenty of time to feel sorry for myself while

I was having all sorts of surgery on my most personal places,' he said with a slightly awkward laugh.

And yet he'd been married, so... 'You must have had a good surgeon,' she said, and he nodded.

'Yeah, I did. An excellent surgeon, but even he couldn't rescue me entirely. You could say I discovered the concept of self-preservation the hard way.'

Her mind pictured a young man on the brink of adulthood facing weeks or months of rehabilitation and the news that his life would be changed for ever just because of a foolish stunt that had gone horribly wrong. 'That's a tough lesson to learn,' she said, watching the laughter fading from his face.

'It was, but it could have been a lot worse. My surgeon's one of the reasons I went into medicine. I contemplated a career in urology for a bit.'

'And then you went into general practice.'

'Yes. Because it offers variety and a more flexible career path, and I wanted to be there for Samuel. I owed it to him, and to my parents, and I could be closer to them that way. And I'm OK. Well, apart from the kids, but I've come to terms with that. I thought Rachel had, too, but she left me when Samuel was getting worse and I was on call to my parents more and more often, because she'd met someone else.'

'She left you *then*? When you really needed support? Nick, that's awful!'

'It happens, though. Your husband left you when you were pregnant.'

'Yes, well, we won't talk about him,' she said, dismissing him and picking up another chocolate. 'So, did Rachel have children with this new man?'

'Yes. She was pregnant when she left me, and of course there was no way it could be mine, not without IVF.'

'IVF? So that's still an option?'

'Yeah. There was a chance they could aspirate some viable sperm cells from the undamaged tissue if we'd really wanted to try for children, but it meant IVF with all the drugs and stuff, so it wouldn't be easy and there were no guarantees, and she wasn't interested in doing that. She'd had a friend who'd had a horrendous experience, and it freaked her out so she wouldn't consider it.'

'And that's the only way?'

'Oh, yes. The tubes were shredded beyond repair, so I am well and truly firing blanks.'

Her brain was still processing what he'd told her when she opened her mouth.

'So I guess that means it all still works otherwise?' she asked without thinking, and he started to laugh as she felt her face burn up. She buried it in her hands and met his eyes over her fingertips. 'I can't believe I said that. Oh, I'm so sorry—'

He shook his head slowly, his eyes laughing. 'Oh, no, don't be, it's worth it just to see your face. And, yes, it does all still work, thank you for your concern.'

He grinned, his eyes alight with mischief now. 'My mother found that out. She came into the bathroom and caught me doing what teenage boys do a lot, and she went pink, said, "Well, that answers that question," and shut the door behind her. I thought I was going to die of embarrassment, and I didn't leave the bathroom for well over an hour.'

She bit her lip, but the laugh wouldn't stay inside and they ended up in stitches.

'Sorry. I know it isn't really funny, but...'

'It sort of is. Didn't feel it at the time, but I can laugh about it now.'

'So. you must have been very lucky—either that or the surgeon was particularly brilliant. I can't believe you got away with it. That's amazing.'

'It is. Want to check it out?'

She met his eyes, startled, and for a breathless moment neither of them said anything, but then he grinned and leant back with another chocolate, and she saw the twinkle in his eyes.

'I think I'll pass, if that's OK,' she said with a smile, but her heart was pounding and all she could see was that crisp white linen at the far end of the house and she wanted him like she'd never wanted anyone before.

*Why had he said that?*

Just when it was all going well and everything seemed fine and comfortable between them, he went and messed it up.

That weird thing with his heart again, and although he'd only been joking, he kind of hadn't been. Not really.

Not that he'd have expected her to say yes, but he certainly wouldn't have turned her down. He'd probably put her off with all the gory stuff.

He swung his legs off the sofa and got to his feet. 'I'm sure I'll get over it. Fancy another coffee?'

She shook her head and stood up, still looking a little flustered. 'No, I—I ought to go home. Things to do.'

'At eleven o'clock on a Friday night?'

She looked at her watch, more for something to do than to tell the time, he thought, and then looked back up at him.

'Nick, I...' She let out a shaky breath and walked past him down the stairs and stopped at the door. 'I need to go.'

He followed her down and stopped an arm's length away from her, just for safety's sake, and met her eyes. They were filled with all sorts of things he couldn't begin to analyse, but rejection wasn't one of them.

'You don't, not if you don't want to. I wasn't hitting on you, Ellie, but I'd be more than happy if you wanted to stay. Truly.'

Their eyes locked, and for what felt like hours but was probably only seconds, neither of them breathed. And then she took a tiny step towards him, then another one.

'It's really not a good idea,' she said, her voice thready, her breath soft against his face.

'No, it probably isn't.' He lifted a hand and stroked his knuckles down her cheek, then turned his hand and dragged his thumb slowly over her dry lips. She flicked her tongue out to moisten them, and his breath hitched in his throat and he swallowed.

'Stay with me, Ellie,' he said gruffly, and with a broken little sigh she stepped into his arms and lifted her face up to his.

# CHAPTER FOUR

HIS STRONG HANDS cradled her face gently as
his head came down to meet hers, his mouth
warm and supple.

His touch was delicate, but it seemed to
reach every nerve cell in her body. She felt
the tender caress of his fingertips against her
cheeks, the heat of his tongue as he stroked
her lips, tracing the tiny gap between them,
and she parted them and felt his breath fill her
mouth before his tongue claimed it.

He tasted of coffee and chocolate with a
hint of mint, and his kiss was sure and slow,
searching, tempting. She heard a tiny sound—
hers?—and he let go of her face and eased her
body up against his, letting out a low groan as
they came into contact from top to toe.

'You feel so good,' he whispered, rock-
ing his hips against hers, and she squeezed
her legs together to soothe the raging need as
one hand slid round and cradled her breast,

the other pressing her closer, lifting her hard against him so she felt the unmistakable jut of his erection against her body.

'OK, you didn't lie,' she said breathlessly, to defuse the tension, and she felt the soft huff of his laughter in her mouth.

'I think it probably needs a more thorough examination,' he murmured, and the smile in his voice made her laugh.

'Oh, definitely, but maybe standing by a glass door with the light on isn't the best place for it,' she mumbled, and he laughed again and eased away from her, his eyes oddly intense as the smile faded and the heat ramped up again.

'Come to bed,' he murmured, and she nodded and watched him swallow, the tension like a tight cord between them as he took her hand and led her down the corridor to his bedroom. He closed the door and turned back the covers, but he didn't put on the light. He didn't need to, because the room was flooded with moonlight, slanting across the floor and highlighting every plane of his face, leaving his eyes in shadow.

He held out his hand and led her to the bed, then cupped her face again in gentle fingers that weren't quite steady.

'I want you so much,' he said quietly. 'I've

wanted to touch you, to hold you, since you let rip at me in Reception.'

'I have no idea why, I was horribly rude,' she said, feeling another wash of shame about the way she'd behaved, but he just smiled, and as he tipped his head on one side there was a twinkle in his eyes that could have been the moonlight, but she didn't think so.

'You were, but you were outrageously beautiful with it.' His fingers traced her face, the touch making her nerve endings dance as his hands moved slowly lower, his fingers finding the hem of her top and sliding up under it.

She sucked in her breath, pulling her postbaby tummy in, and she saw him frown as he stroked the skin with his warm hand.

'Why are you doing that? Relax. You're beautiful, Ellie.'

'I'm flabby.'

'No. You've had three children. Be proud of your body and what it's achieved. It's amazing. Such a gift. Don't ever feel ashamed of that.'

And just like that, he took away her worries, the niggle of fear that he wouldn't want her when he'd seen her, and freed her to be herself.

'I think you're wearing too much,' she said to him, suddenly braver, and he laughed again and took a step back.

'I think we're both wearing too much,' he

said with a smile, and pulled his sweater over his head, hooked his thumbs in his waistband and shucked off his jeans and underwear in one.

'Better?' he asked, and she just stared at him, at the fit, honed body that clearly wanted hers, the strong, straight legs, the board-flat abs, the deep chest and powerful shoulders, and felt another wave of doubt.

'Hey,' he murmured, a little frown pleating his brow again, and he stepped closer again and touched her face. 'Do you want me to close the curtains?'

She shook her head. 'No. I'm just being a coward.'

'Then let me help you,' he said quietly, and took hold of the hem of her top and lifted it up and over her head, dropping it on the floor with his clothes. He undid the button on her jeans and tugged them down inch by inch, his mouth tracing down over her ribs, her stomach—sucked in again—and then pausing.

'Lacy knickers,' he said with a smile, and left them there while he stripped off her jeans, impatient now. 'Lift up,' he instructed, and eased them off one foot at a time, then straightened and pulled her up against him. 'That's better,' he murmured, and his mouth found hers again in a gentle kiss.

Except it wasn't gentle, not for long. She felt his fractured sigh in her mouth and gave a tiny whimper in response, and that was enough. With a ragged groan he cradled the back of her head with one hand, hauled her hard up against him and plundered her mouth, his tongue delving, searching, duelling with hers as they rocked against each other, their bodies striving for more.

'I need you,' he breathed, the air shuddering from his body, and she felt her legs turn to jelly.

'I need you, too,' she told him, and then they were on the bed in a tangle of arms and legs and desperate, seeking hands, their mouths locked together as their bodies found each other. Her underwear was gone, his hands on every inch of her, so clever, so knowing.

'Now, Nick, please...'

She gasped as he entered her, caught his groan in her mouth and they stilled, letting sensation wash over them.

'Ah, that feels so good,' he said after the longest moment, and then he kissed her again and started to move. She met him thrust for thrust, her body arching into his, touching him everywhere she could reach while his hands sought out all her sweet spots as if he knew her better than she knew herself.

She felt the tension building, her hands clawing at him now, begging, pleading, and then she was there, wave after wave of sensation crashing over her as his body stiffened and he surged into her one last time.

Then the tension drained from them both, and he sagged against her, a soft huff of laughter teasing her skin as he rolled to his side and took her with him, his chest rising and falling as his breathing slowed and returned to normal. He lifted a hand and smoothed the hair off her face and then kissed her, a lingering brush of his lips before he let out a long, heartfelt sigh and smiled, his eyes tender.

'That was amazing,' he murmured, sifting her hair with his fingers, his smile contented.

She smiled back and lifted her hand to cradle his jaw, the slight graze of stubble prickling her palm.

'It was. I think I love your surgeon.'

He chuckled, a deep rumble in his chest, and rolled onto his back with a long, drawn-out sigh.

She propped herself up on one elbow and studied his body, stretched out in the moonlight in all its glory. 'You had an ex-fix on your pelvis,' she said, tracing the little silver scars on his hipbones with a fingertip.

'Mmm. I had one on my ankle, as well, until they were able to rebuild it.'

'Is that why you limp sometimes? Your ankle?'

He nodded. 'It doesn't like the cold. I tried an ice bath once just to see what it was like, and it was excruciating. There's a ton of scaffolding in it, but hey. At least I still have my foot. I nearly didn't.'

She felt her eyes widen. 'It was that bad? You really did trash yourself, didn't you?'

'Oh, yeah.' His smile was wry. 'I don't think my parents have ever got over it.'

'Do they know why you did it?'

He nodded again, his smile fading. 'I don't remember telling them, but they gave me some pretty fancy drugs in hospital and apparently I blurted it all out and gave them a massive guilt trip. I just thought—I don't know what I thought. Maybe I'd fall off my bike as it landed and I'd break my arm, or scrape myself on the ground and get a load of bruises. I never in a million years imagined just how badly I'd hurt myself, but as I lay there getting all that attention, there was a moment when I thought it had been worth it.'

'But not now.'

'Oh, no. Absolutely not, and the feeling didn't last long. I was an idiot, and I suppose

I got what I deserved, but you know, I was a kid, and my judgement was flawed. We all make mistakes, but most of them don't hurt that much. Not just me, but everyone, and most particularly Samuel. That was what really hurt me, more than anything else.'

She stared at him, horrified. 'Did they tell him why you did it?'

'No. He guessed. He cried when he saw me, and told me I didn't want to be like him, but while I lay there helpless for weeks I got a taste of what he went through all the time, and it changed me for the better. I suppose in a way it was worth it, just for that, to make me a better person. And there was plenty of room for improvement.'

She felt her eyes prickle for the boy he'd been, so desperate for someone to notice he was struggling, too kind to say so until it all got too much. She lay down again beside him, wrapping her arm around his waist, his arm around her shoulders as she laid her head on his chest and listened to the slow, steady beat of his heart. She felt the touch of his lips on her hair, the warm drift of his breath against her cheek.

'I'm OK, Ellie. Truly. It was more than half my life ago. I've made my peace with it and it's over now.'

Was it? Was it really? She wasn't sure. She tilted her head back and tried to read his eyes, but the moon had gone behind a thin wisp of cloud and she couldn't see him clearly any more.

He kissed her briefly, then pulled away and swung his legs over the side of the bed. 'I need to take Rufus out for a minute and then settle him in his bed. Mind your eyes,' he murmured, and reached out and turned on the bedside lamp and started to pull on his clothes.

She watched him, seeing the scars now in the lamp light, his left leg a mishmash of fine lines, the ankle slightly thicker.

*At least I've still got my foot.*

'Are you taking him for a walk?'

'Yes. Not far, just out onto the lane and down to the top of the steps so he can have a bit of a sniff around before he goes to bed. I won't be long.'

'I should go home,' she said, not really wanting to but not wanting to outstay her welcome.

He turned back to her. 'Really?'

She shrugged. 'I haven't got my toothbrush,' she said, which sounded pathetic as it came out of her mouth, but it was the only thing she could come up with, and he gave a soft huff of laughter and sat back down on the edge of the bed, dropping a kiss on her lips.

'I'm sure we can get round that. Please stay.'

It was the 'please' that did it, that and the look in his eyes which told her clearly that he meant it.

'OK,' she said softly, and he kissed her again.

'Keep the bed warm for me,' he said, and went out, leaving the door open.

She heard him walking briskly down the corridor, calling Rufus, heard the jingle of his collar and the sound of the front door closing, and she slipped out of bed to investigate the bathroom.

Did she have time for a shower before he got back? Maybe. She turned on the shower, stepped into the stream of hot water and reached for the shower gel. It smelt of him, the smell that had tantalised her all week, and as she smoothed it over her body she felt the caress of his hands, the touch of his mouth, the warmth of his arms around her.

Fantasy was a wonderful thing.

He heard water running, and settling Rufus with a biscuit he went back to his bedroom, closing the door in case the dog got any ideas.

She was in the shower, and he stripped off his clothes and went into the bathroom to join her.

'That seems like a good idea,' he said, sliding his arms around her from behind.

'Oh! You made me jump,' she said, turning and smiling up at him, and he smoothed the damp hair away from her face and found her mouth with his.

'Sorry,' he murmured. 'I just couldn't resist it.'

'You're too late, I'm done,' she said sadly, and he smiled.

'That's a shame, but I'm not,' he told her, then held his arms out to the side, his smile mischievous. 'Well, go on, then. You know you want to.'

So she did. She explored every inch of his body with soapy hands, driving him crazy with every touch and leaving the best till last. Her hand closed around him and he shut his eyes, his breath hissing out as she stroked him firmly but annoyingly slowly.

'You're killing me.'

'Mmm. Maybe it's time to move this somewhere more comfortable,' she said, and reached for a towel, leaving him to rinse.

He wasn't far behind her...

She went home after breakfast, but only long enough to do some laundry and tidy up a bit, and then she went back to his house with a change of clothes and her toothbrush, and they spent the weekend doing nothing.

Well, not nothing. They walked Rufus along the beach and had lunch in the Harbour Inn down by the river, and then went back to his house and made love lazily all afternoon until, as he put it, she'd checked out all his scars and satisfied herself that everything worked. And then checked again...

He threw together a tasty pasta dish for supper, and they ate it on their knees in front of the television, then walked Rufus again before going back to bed, and the next day they got in the car and drove to Dunwich Heath and took Rufus for a longer walk with lots of things to sniff, then had lunch in the café and got back in the car to drive back to Yoxburgh.

Back to reality, she thought, and realised that for the first time ever, she hadn't thought about the children all day, and that made her feel sick with guilt.

She was quiet in the car, a little unresponsive, the light-hearted banter of their weekend suddenly absent.

'What's wrong?' he asked, when she'd been silent for a while.

She shrugged. 'Nothing.'

'Yeah, there is. Come on, talk to me. Don't bottle things up. We need to be honest with each other, Ellie. If my stupidity taught me nothing else, it taught me that.'

She shrugged again. 'I just feel guilty.'

'Because of David? Tell me not, please.'

She stared at him for a second as if he was mad, and shook her head with a quiet laugh. 'No. Absolutely not because of David. I have no guilt where he's concerned.'

'Good.' He searched her eyes for a moment, then he slowed the car and pulled over to the side of the road in a little layby on the edge of some woods and cut the engine, undoing his seat belt and shifting so he was facing her.

'What happened, Ellie? Why did he leave you when you were pregnant?'

She sighed and looked away, staring blankly out of the windscreen. He had no idea what he was seeing in her head, but it didn't seem to be making her very happy.

'He didn't believe the baby was his,' she said softly after a pause so long he wondered if it would ever end. 'He was away a lot—an awful lot, and he came back after being gone for nearly three months and of course as usual the first thing he wanted was to go to bed, but we didn't have any condoms, and I wasn't using oral contraception because I was still breastfeeding Oscar, so I said no, and he said it was fine anyway, while he'd been away he'd had the vasectomy he'd been talking about so I couldn't get pregnant.'

'But you did.'

She nodded. 'Yes. I did. And when he came back six weeks later I'd done a test because I'd missed a period and it was positive, so I told him we were having another baby and he said it couldn't possibly be his.'

He frowned, because it didn't add up. 'But—surely he'd been tested? Didn't it occur to him to go back to the clinic and get them to check their results?'

'There were no results,' she said flat, her voice oddly flat. 'He hadn't been back for the tests—too busy, apparently. But he still didn't believe it could be his, because they'd told him he'd be fine. Or so he said. So he told me he wanted me to have a termination, and I refused. I hadn't really wanted him to have a vasectomy anyway, but he didn't want any more children, and he said he certainly didn't want someone else's. I said he could hardly blame me if I *had* found someone else, as he left me alone so much. So he walked out.'

'That's what happened with me and Rachel. I was never there, so she found someone who was. It's not unheard of.'

She shrugged. 'I know, but I didn't do that. Anyway, he took it as an admission of guilt and walked out. His parting shot was that he said he wasn't supporting another man's child. Then I got his mother on the phone, begging me to get a DNA test to prove the child's paternity, and I refused, because I knew perfectly well who the father was, so he divorced me on grounds of adultery.'

'And you didn't contest it?'

'I couldn't be bothered, and anyway life was easier without him. So he divorced me, put the house in my name and he pays me maintenance, and when Evie was born she was the spitting image of the other two, of course. None of them look like me, so they're either all his or none of them are, but he wouldn't hear it.'

'Couldn't he see the resemblance?' he asked, deciding the man was an idiot and hoping he never got to meet him, and she turned and gave him a tired smile.

'Probably, but I think pride got in his way. Anyway, his mother had the test done without telling me, which made me furious, but of course then he had proof that he was wrong, and he wanted to come back.'

'And you said no.'

'I did. He didn't trust me at the time, he didn't believe me, he accused me of committing adultery and he's never apologised because that would mean he'd have to admit he was in the wrong, and he'll never do that. He says I misled him, implied I'd had an affair, which I hadn't, I'd just said that he could hardly blame me if I had. Anyway, he now accepts Evie's his, and he has all of them at the weekends, and he does his best to be a good father but we don't always agree on how he does that.'

'Does he spoil them?'

'Always. They have what they want, which isn't good for them, but hey. He has them, he maintains contact, and they need that so I just deal with the fallout and mitigate it where I can.'

'What about his parents? What do they think?'

'Oh, they're furious with him for walking away from his family without establishing the facts, but they support him and they've always known Evie's his. Liz just wanted to prove it to him, which she's done, and although I was cross it was probably the right thing to do and at least he now acknowledges her.'

He nodded slowly. 'OK, so that's David out of the way, so why are you feeling guilty? Why now, today? Because of us?'

She shrugged again, her shoulders shifting a fraction in defeat. 'Because of us doing this.

Having fun. I haven't thought about them once all day, Nick. What kind of a mother does that make me?'

'A perfectly normal one. Your children are safe, you know that. You're just having me time, and you're entitled to do that, surely?'

'It just seems wrong.'

'Why? You have a right to be you.'

'But I'm not being me. *Me* is the mother of three children, not...'

'Not the warm, generous, vibrant woman who's spent the last two nights in my bed making love with me? Making me laugh, making me smile? You can be both, Ellie. Sure, you're a mother, but you're also a woman, and you're entitled to feelings that don't revolve around your children. Time to be yourself, to do the other things that make you who you are. We can still do that.'

She shook her head. 'How? I have every other weekend, that's all, at best, and sometimes not even that. My time without them is so short, but I don't really want them to form a relationship with you, because when it goes wrong they'll be hurt and I don't want that for them, and anyway that's not what this is about, and it's not like they need a father figure, so that cuts out any other time.'

'So we'll have every other weekend when we can, and we'll make it special, and that's fine. It's fine with me, at least. I'm not a hormonal teenager, Ellie. I can do deferred gratification without getting all stroppy and demanding. It's about quality, not quantity. I'm not going to behave like a spoilt brat if I don't get to see you one weekend, either.'

Unlike David, who'd apparently wanted every second of her attention every time he'd seen fit to come back into her life for a few days before jetting off back to his real world. He didn't say that, though, just left her to fill in the gaps.

'I know you're not like that, but you deserve more,' she said, her voice oddly choked all of a sudden, but he shook his head.

'I don't *want* more than that, Ellie. I don't need you twenty-four seven. And wonderful though I'm sure they are, I don't need to be part of your children's lives. They've got a father, as you've pointed out, and I've done standing in for the real father with my own sisters and it didn't go well. Really, I'm fine with it. It suits me. I'm pretty self-sufficient. I don't mind being alone. I like it. It makes a refreshing change after a lifetime of caring, believe me.'

She turned her head and searched his face, and he held her eyes and smiled.

'Are you sure?' she asked, and he nodded.

'Yes, Ellie. I'm sure. We'll get together when we can, and it'll be fine.'

'But—what if it's not enough?'

'It will be.'

'But what if it's *not*? What if we want more?'

'Then we'll cross that bridge if we get to it,' he said, and leant over and cupped her chin in his hand and kissed her gently. 'Don't worry, Ellie. We'll make it work. Maybe not always, but as often as we can.'

'Are you sure? Sometimes he's away for four or five weeks at a time.'

He smiled and kissed her again. 'Then we'll have to find another way. And anyhow, we'll see each other every day at work.'

'Three days. I only work three days.'

'Even so. Don't worry, Ellie. It'll be fine.'

He gave her a reassuring smile, restarted the engine and drove back to his house.

'Tea?'

She shook her head. 'No, Nick, I need to go home. I'm not sure what time Liz will bring them back. It varies between four thirty and well after their bedtime, and they never tell me. I think he must imagine I hang myself up on a hook in the hall cupboard and wait for them to come home.'

He chuckled and drew her into his arms. 'Go on, then. You go home to your hook, and I'll see you in the morning. I'll walk so you can have the parking place, just in case they're on the drag tomorrow. I think the forecast is rain anyway and you don't all need to get drenched.'

'You're such a star,' she said, looking up into his eyes, and they creased with his smile.

'I aim to please,' he murmured, and kissed her lingeringly, then lifted his head and stared down at her. 'Go home, Ellie, before I cart you off to bed and make you late.'

Oh, she was so tempted to let him. 'I wish,' she said with a tired huff of laughter, and then she laid her palm against his cheek. 'Thank you, Nick—for everything. It's been such a lovely weekend. I don't remember when I last laughed so much.'

His smile touched her heart. 'No. Nor do I. It's been amazing.' He kissed her again, and let her go with a reluctant smile. 'Go on, go home. I'll call you later.'

'Don't call. Text me, just in case they're late. I might be putting them to bed still.'

He nodded, and she picked up the bag with her change of clothes in it and made her way home, the warmth of his smile wrapped around her heart.

'Mummy, Mummy, look what Daddy got us!'

She frowned at the two tablets in their child-proof, supposedly indestructible cases, and met Liz's eyes over their heads.

'I thought we had an agreement about this stuff?' she said under her breath, trying to keep a lid on her frustration. 'They're too young for electronic devices, David knows that. It's not good for their developmental skills. If he wants to entertain them, he needs to try talking to them.'

'But you know what they're like, Ellie. All Maisie talks about is unicorns and mermaids, and Oscar just wants to run about pretending to be an aeroplane. He doesn't know where to start.'

'So get him to talk about unicorns and aeroplanes! Or take them to the park, or soft play or something, instead of buying them expensive electronic babysitters so he can spend the whole weekend on his phone checking on his investments!'

'He doesn't do that,' Liz protested weakly, but she knew better and said so.

'I lived with him for five years, Liz. I *know* what he's like.' She shifted the sleepy baby to her other hip and eyed her mother-in-law steadily over Evie's head. 'What did he get Evie?'

She looked awkward. 'He didn't. Even he agrees she's too young for a tablet. And I did ask, Ellie, but he's not easy to reason with and he doesn't really understand babies.'

She stifled a growl of anger and called the children. 'Come and say goodbye to Grandma, please. And say thank you for your presents and having you for the weekend.'

It took a minute more before she could close the door behind her and let out the sigh of frustration. There was a scream locked up behind it, but she kept that under control and took them into the sitting room and put Evie down on the floor with a box of her toys.

'Mummy, I can't do this unicorn game!' Maisie wailed, but the wail only increased when she took the machines away from her and Oscar and told them they'd be rationed to half an hour a day maximum, and only at the weekends.

She asked them what they'd done with their

father, and from what she could glean it was not a lot apart from the wretched electronic devices, which he'd *known* she didn't want them to have. By the time she got them all to sleep that night it was almost ten o'clock, and she was exhausted and even crosser, if that was possible.

She was sitting down with a coffee wondering how the judge might react if she killed him when she heard the message tone on her phone.

Nick, as promised.

How are things?

She snorted softly and wrote, He got them tablets. Not pharma, obvs. I might have to kill him.

Oh, dear. Best not. Not great for your career... Want to talk?

She rang him, and just the sound of his voice was enough to calm her fury.

'Why did he do it?' she asked, frustrated. 'He knows what I think. We've had this conversation several times. He just ignores me and goes over my head.'

'So take them away and tell them they can only have them when they're with him. Simple.'

That made her laugh. 'I can tell you haven't met my children,' she said. 'And anyway, that's not the worst of it. The thing I'm most angry about is that he didn't get Evie anything at all. It's like she doesn't exist.'

'How old is she?'

'Fifteen months—and I know she doesn't know what she's missing, but it won't be long. She's his, too, for heaven's sake, and he knows that now. Why can't he treat them equally? I just wish…'

'What? That he was a reasonable human being? That you were a better judge of character? Don't go there. I've been through all of this with Rachel, all the "what ifs", and if you let it, it'll eat you alive. Deal with the tablets, ration the screen time, put up with the protests. They'll get over it, although it'll probably take a while. And buy something nice for Evie.'

She could hear the smile in his voice, and the sympathy, and she sighed and settled back against the sofa.

'You're such a reasonable human being.'

'I wasn't always. Maybe he just needs to learn the hard way, whatever that is.'

'If only. I'm sorry, it's not fair of me to un-load on you, especially after such a lovely weekend,' she said wistfully. 'Thank you so much for going to so much trouble for me. It was like living out a fantasy. Just idyllic.'

'Hey,' he murmured, his voice soft. 'Don't sound so sad. We can do it again in two weeks. And anyway, it was no trouble, I seem to re-member I wasn't exactly left out of the fun.'

'I just wish it wasn't over. Don't get me wrong, I love my babies to bits, but it was just so nice to be the other me for a while.'

'I know. So what are you doing now?' he asked.

'Lying on the sofa, drinking coffee.'

'Decaf?'

She smiled wearily. 'Don't worry, it won't keep me awake. For some reason I don't seem to have had very much sleep this weekend.'

'I wonder why that could be?' he asked, and she could picture his lazy, sexy smile.

'I can't imagine,' she murmured back, and then yawned hugely. 'Oh, sorry, I really am pooped. I need to go to bed.'

'Me, too. Rufus is out for the count. I think that walk at Dunwich was a bit long for him. It was lovely, though. We ought to do it again when the heather's out.'

'We should.'

She yawned again, and he laughed and said goodnight and she put her phone on charge and headed up to bed, still frustrated about the tablets but wrapped around now by the sound of Nick's voice and the warmth of his smile.

And in two weeks' time, they could do it all over again…

# CHAPTER FIVE

'MORNING! KETTLE'S HOT.'

And not just the kettle. His voice was bright and breezy, but his eyes across the busy staff room held a different and far more personal message, and she felt her breath hitch. This was going to be much harder than she'd thought.

'Morning!'

She'd conjured up her best cheery voice, to match his, and she picked up her mug and gave him what she hoped would look like a friendly and professional smile as she reached for the teabags. 'Thank you for leaving me the parking space. The thought of trying to frog-march the children to nursery in the pouring rain is enough to bring me out in hives. I hope you didn't get soaked?'

'Only a bit. Don't worry, I'm pretty water-proof. So, how were the little darlings today?'

She rolled her eyes, and he grinned.

'*That* good.'

'Oh, yeah. They were overtired, overstimulated by the electronics and properly grumpy last night, and they're not much better today. I don't envy nursery.'

He lowered his voice a fraction. 'Sounds like you haven't forgiven him yet.'

'Absolutely not. I swear he does it just to annoy me.' She turned round with her tea in her hand and smiled at the others. 'So, how's the day looking? Has the entire population of Yoxburgh gone down with the plague?'

Lucy chuckled and got to her feet. 'Maybe not the whole population, but the phone hasn't stopped ringing so we'll all be pretty busy, I think. Better go and make a start if I want to get home tonight.'

'Yeah, me, too,' Nick said from behind her, and touched her back discreetly. 'See you later.'

Much later, as it turned out, because the phone didn't stop ringing and while they didn't have the plague, what seemed like half their patient list apparently needed urgent appointments, and her surgery list was huge.

*Please let them be nice, simple, straightforward cases.*

Or not. The first was fine, but her second patient of the day was an asthmatic who was disturbingly short of breath. She gave him oxygen and medication and got Megan, one of the nursing team, to monitor him, but three patients later she had a call from her to say he was deteriorating, so she checked on him again and phoned the hospital, spoke to Lucy's husband Andy in the ED at Yoxburgh Park Hospital, and the patient's wife took him straight over there. It was the easiest and quickest thing to do, as the hospital was just across the park from the practice and it would save waiting for an ambulance and get him seen quicker.

She went back to her patients, only to be interrupted again by a call about a deteriorating terminally ill patient who urgently needed end-of-life medication. She said she'd authorise it and visit him as soon as she could get away, then called the pharmacist. It only took five minutes to sort out, but it was yet another interruption, and it was after twelve before she had time to review her pharmacy queries, deal with the sick note requests and make calls to patients who'd requested phone consultations.

She went up to the staff room at five past one and found them all gathered round having their daily catch-up and signing repeat prescriptions. Lucy handed her a stack for her own patients, and she sat down and worked her way through them as fast as she could.

A coffee appeared in front of her, and she glanced up and met Nick's sympathetic eyes.

'Oh, you're a star. Thank you.'

'My pleasure,' he murmured, and hooked out the chair opposite her and sat down. 'Can I have ten seconds?'

Really? She put her pen down and met his eyes again. 'Sure. Fire away.'

'I've just seen one of your patients—Judith Granger. She's seen you a couple of times with query irritable bowel, but it's flared up over the weekend and she's feeling very tired and a bit breathless, and I'm a bit worried there's something more going on. She's lost weight, and she says it's probably because she's been too busy to eat as much and she hasn't been that hungry, but she seemed quite happy about it.'

'And you're not?'

He shook his head. 'She's lost several pounds in the last two months, but it's the tiredness that brought her in, and she looks tired, too. Tired and drained and a bit anaemic.'

'You're thinking bowel cancer?'

'Maybe. I've sent her off to the lab for blood tests and a faecal sample, and we'll see what comes back, but I think she needs an urgent referral to the colorectal team for further investigation. I just thought I should give you a heads-up.'

She nodded slowly. 'Yes. Thank you. So when did I see her last? Did I miss this?'

'No, I don't think so. You saw her four months ago, and the weight loss has all happened since then, and she said she wasn't too bad until the weekend.'

'Any blood?'

'Not that she noticed, apparently. Anyway, I told her I'd fill you in.'

'OK. Thanks. I'll look out for the results.'

He nodded and went back to his pile of prescriptions, and she put Judith out of her mind and went back to her own, eating the odd bite of her lunch as she worked, but then just as she was about to leave she had a call from the nurse with her terminal patient to say that he'd died quite suddenly.

She was gutted. She'd wanted to see him, to be there for his wife as much as him, and now it was too late. Damn, damn, damn. 'OK, I'll come now,' she said, and stifled a sigh.

'House call?' he murmured, and she met his eyes and nodded.

'Yes, I've got to certify a death.'

'Want me to go?'

She shook her head. 'No. Thank you, but no. He was my patient and I've built a relationship with him and his wife. It's the last thing I can do for him.'

He nodded, gave her an understanding smile and went back to his admin, and she put her lunch back in the fridge. Maybe she'd get time to finish it later.

'Hi.'

'Hi, you.' He could hear the smile in her voice, a quiet murmur over the phone, and he felt it warm him.

'It sounds very peaceful your end,' he said softly. 'Are you good to talk? Are they in bed?'

'Oh, yes. They were ready for an early night, thank goodness, because the last thing I needed after today was another fight about bedtime.'

'So no fight over the tablets?'

He heard a little chuckle. 'No. I'd hidden them, and I told Liz they couldn't have them except at the weekends for a very limited time, so I don't know if they said anything about them to her but they didn't even mention them to me. I think they were too tired, to be honest. Nursery drains them. They keep them very busy.'

'So how was your widow? Did you ever finish your lunch?'

'No. Well, not till four. And as expected she was sad, resigned, glad it was over for him, a bit numb. She'll be OK, but you know how it is. Even when you know it's coming, it's always so final, and we're never ready for that.'

He thought instantly of Samuel, of how he'd thought he was ready and yet wasn't, when the time came. 'Yeah. Yeah, I know. So how was the rest of your day?'

'Oh, busy, too much to do, not enough time. Yours?'

'Mine?' He stretched out on the sofa, one hand idly fondling the dog's ears, and gave a quiet sigh. 'Much the same as yours, I guess. Busy, not enough time. Your car had gone by the time I left, and I still hadn't finished all the admin, so I'll need to get in early tomorrow and nail it before I start. That'll be a rude awakening for poor old Rufus.'

'So what does he do while you're at work all day? Does someone let him out?'

He glanced at the sleeping dog on his lap, and smiled. 'No, he's got a little dog-flap into the area of garden behind the utility room. There's a bit of grass there and he seems quite happy to pop out when he needs to. He's got toys, and he's used to lying around all day, and he gets plenty of games and cuddles when I'm home. He gets a walk morning and evening, regardless of the weather, and he seems happy enough with that unless it's pouring.'

'I bet he wasn't happy this morning, then,' she said, and he heard the smile in her voice and chuckled.

'Not especially. He has a coat I put on him if I have to walk him in the rain, but he did look at me as if I was mad this morning when I opened the door, and he was more than happy to go back to his blanket when we got home.'

'Poor Rufus,' she murmured, her voice rich with sympathy, and he laughed.

'Poor Rufus nothing. He's on my lap right now and I swear if he could purr he'd be doing it.'

'I know the feeling,' she murmured, and he groaned, the flashback to his bedroom so vivid he felt his heart pound.

'Don't. That's torture, Ellie. I'm trying so hard not to think about our weekend and that *really* doesn't help.'

He heard the rueful chuckle. 'Sorry. I've been doing the same, and I'm not having any joy with it either. I didn't mean to torture you.'

'Good, because our next weekend seems an awfully long way away.'

'Tell me about it, and it's only Monday.

We've got another eleven days to wait,' she said in a wry and slightly despairing voice, and it was his turn to laugh.

'We might have to get creative at work. Lock ourselves in a cupboard or something.'

'Like we have time.'

'Yeah. Ah, well. We'll have to make do with phone sex.'

He heard a splutter of laughter, and he grinned.

'I thought you said you weren't a hormonal teenager?' she said, still laughing, and he chuckled.

'Did I? I might have to retract that.' His smile faded, because it was true, he had said it—said it, and believed it, and it seemed he'd been wrong, because all he could think about was being with her and it was killing him.

'I tell you what,' she said. 'I'll make your life easier and get off the phone. I've got laundry to sort before I can go to bed, and I'm shattered.'

'Yeah, me, too. It was a long day. See you tomorrow. Sweet dreams.'

'You, too.' There was a tiny pause, and for a second he thought she was going to say something else. Something on the lines of 'I love you'? But then the line went dead as she hung up and he felt a curious sensation.

Relief? Or disappointment?

He had no idea, but it was oddly disturbing, whatever it was, and he went to bed wondering exactly what it was she hadn't said.

Judith Granger's results came back, and there was blood in the faecal sample and she was quite severely anaemic.

Nick was in the staff room when she went up there at lunchtime on Friday, and he frowned at her, instantly picking up on something, as he always did.

'You OK?' he asked softly.

'Judith Granger. You were right. I've put in an urgent referral request to the colorectal team. She's got an iron deficiency and they found blood.'

He nodded slowly. 'Doesn't surprise me. Have you told her yet?'

'No. I got Katie to call her and ask her to come in and see me again, and she's got an appointment this afternoon. I don't want her wondering what they've found all weekend. She needs to know—but then of course she'll spend the next couple of weeks until she sees them wondering what they'll find.'

He smiled understandingly and turned o the kettle. 'It's always the way. There's easy way to break bad news, or even to h

at it, but she struck me as someone who'd want answers.'

She nodded. 'Yes, she is. Thank you for picking it up. I'm kicking myself for not chasing it earlier.'

'Hey, you didn't miss anything. I read your notes. They were thorough, and she didn't have any symptoms severe enough to indicate cancer. You haven't let her down, Ellie, and she might not have it. There are all sorts of other things it could be.'

She wasn't convinced, though, and it took Judith herself to point out later that day that things had changed quite rapidly in the past week or so, which made her feel a little better.

'I'm sorry it's not better news, though, Judith,' she told her, but the woman just smiled.

'That's OK, Dr Kendal. I thought you might find something, and in a way I'm glad. At least now I know I wasn't imagining it and I'm not wasting your time.'

'No,' she said vehemently, shaking her head. 'It's never wasting our time if you think something's wrong. You know your body better than anyone. If it's telling you something, there's a reason, and it's far better to get it checked out than to wait until it's too late, and very often it turns out to be something much less significant, as it might well do now. That's

why I've referred you. You should see someone within a week or so.'

'So what will they do?'

She ignored the time pressure and talked
Judith through all the possible diagnostic tests
she might have, the imaging techniques they
could use, and assured her she could come
back at any time if she needed to talk about it.
It put her behind, of course, but that was the
story of her life, and she ended up running to
nursery and collecting the children five minutes late.

And then, because it was the weekend,
all Maisie and Oscar wanted to do was play
games on their tablets, even though Oscar
could hardly understand what he was meant to
do and Maisie was getting increasingly frustrated.

Not as frustrated as she was, and if it wasn't
for the ensuing row it would cause, she would
have put the wretched things in the bin on Saturday morning.

David had a lot to answer for.

She got to her feet. 'Come on, guys. It's
a lovely day. Let's go for a walk along the
beach.'

'I don't want to go for a walk. I want to play
the unicorn game!'

'No. You've done enough, Maisie. It's time for some fresh air and sunshine.'

She rounded them up, put Evie in the back-pack and chivvied Oscar and Maisie into shoes and jumpers, then headed out of the door. And of course once they were out it was fine, the children running along the pavement towards Jacob's Lane because that was the way they *always* went to the beach, with her following.

Would they bump into Nick and Rufus?

Maybe. She wasn't sure if that was a good idea or not. Probably not, but although her mind was telling her that, her heart and her body seemed to have a different view.

They passed the beach huts under the trees at the top of the cliff, then the houses beyond them set back from the road towards the cliff edge, and then they were there, turning onto the small gravelled road that led past his house and round the corner to the top of the steps.

There was no sign of him at the house, although she looked up at his sitting room windows on the way past just in case, and she felt a twinge of disappointment.

Stupid. Why did she want to see him when she was smothered in children? Unless she wanted to put him off her completely, of course. Not that she wanted a relationship with him that included the children because, as he'd pointed out, they had a father, and even if he was an idiot, he was still their father and they didn't need another one.

*Oh, why's it so complicated?*

And then she turned round to see where the children were, and he was there, rounding the corner, Rufus trotting happily beside him, his ears and undercarriage sopping wet, his tongue lolling. He caught sight of her and came running, ears flying, lead trailing, and she bent down and made a fuss of him.

'Morning.'

She looked up—past sodden trainers, up long legs clad in dripping jeans, to a smiling face.

'You got them away from the tablets, then,' he murmured, and she straightened up and smiled at him a little self-consciously.

'Yes. I thought I'd drag them out for some fresh air.' She glanced down at his wet legs. 'It looks like you got caught in the surf,' she added, and he gave her a rueful grin.

'Yeah, that wasn't planned. I saw a wave coming and grabbed Rufus before he got washed away. He doesn't mind wet feet, but he panics if he's out of his depth and it's a bit rough today, but it was quite chilly. So this must be Evie. Hi, Evie,' he said, smiling over her shoulder at the baby in the backpack, and she turned and scanned the lane for the others.

'Kids, where are you?' she said, feeling a moment of panic, but then she heard a giggle and there they were, tucked behind a shrub in the entrance to his drive, hiding, and the breath left her lungs in a rush.

'Monkeys. Come here!' She turned back to him. 'Sorry about that. They don't understand the laws of trespass.'

He chuckled and looked round as the children emerged from the undergrowth and ran up to them.

'Who are you?' Maisie asked, looking up at him curiously, and Ellie's heart sank. This was not meant to happen!

'I'm Nick. Who are you?'

'I'm Maisie, and this is Oscar. Why are you talking to Mummy?'

She dived in fast. 'Nick's a doctor, too, and he's just started working in Yoxburgh, so I know him.'

'Are you at Mummy's work?' Maisie asked, studying him intently, and he nodded.

'Yes, I am.'

'Is she your friend?' Oscar asked him.

She saw his mouth twitch. 'Well, sort of. We see each other at work a lot and I suppose you could say we were friends. We're colleagues, really.'

'Collies? Like the dogs?'

She rescued him before it got any worse. 'Not collies, Maisie. Colleagues. That means people you work with. It's like I work with Lucy and Dev and the others,' she explained. Except of course it wasn't, not anything like it…

'Can you fly a plane?' Oscar asked out of the blue, and Nick laughed and shook his head.

'No, I'm afraid not.'

'My daddy can,' Maisie said proudly, and Ellie frowned.

'I don't think he can.'

'He says he can. He's got a friend with a plane and she lets him fly it. What's your dog called?' she asked, moving on abruptly as children did and leaving Ellie wondering who the friend with the plane was. And…*she*?

Not that David's friendships or private life were any of her business, any more than hers were his business, and besides, coming from Maisie it was as likely as not all a work of fiction.

'His name's Rufus,' Nick told Maisie, and met her eyes over the children's heads. 'Fancy a quick coffee?'

'Oh. Um—we were heading to the beach—'

'Can we have a snack?' Oscar asked, looking remarkably like Rufus when he was begging, and Nick's lips twitched again.

'That's up to your mother, but I'm sure I could find you something if she says it's OK.'

''Nack,' Evie said from behind her ear, and before she knew it they were all inside his house and the children were clustered round him as he investigated the contents of a cupboard.

'For a doctor, you have an astonishing collection of unwholesome rubbish,' she said drily, and he grinned at her.

'Don't I just?' he said unrepentantly, and pulled out a giant packet of crisps.

Not that unwholesome, though, she realised when he handed them to her and went to change, because they were lightly salted and oven baked, and he'd also dug out a punnet of blueberries and put them on the table.

Two minutes later he was back in dry clothes and they were kneeling up on his dining chairs with a little bowl of crisps, a handful of blueberries and a drink of water each, and Rufus, who obviously had a great understanding of small people, had stationed himself between Oscar and Evie, as if he knew they were the most likely to drop things.

'He's not stupid,' Nick said drily, noticing what she was looking at, and she laughed.

'No, I can see that. He's definitely an opportunist.'

'He's also on a diet, but he's nearly down to what he ought to weigh. Mum and Dad were spoiling him a bit.'

'I can imagine. It must have been hard for them, the last year or so.'

He gave a soft snort and poured hot water into the cafetière. 'Try thirty-nine years. They don't quite know what to do with themselves now, but the grandchildren keep them busy.'

'Little people have a way of doing that.'

'Tell me about it.' He pressed the plunger and handed her a coffee, and they stood side by side leaning against the worktop and watching the children eat while they munched on the left-over crisps.

'Where are your parents?' he asked quietly. 'You haven't mentioned them.'

'Oxfordshire—well, my father is. I don't see him very often. My mother died when I was fifteen, and since he got married again it just doesn't feel like home any more.'

'When was that?'

'When I was nineteen? I was away at uni, and I came home for the summer and the whole house was redecorated and all trace of my mother was gone. The only room left untouched was mine, but he'd let her do everything else.'

And it had hurt. Hurt so much that she hadn't gone home again for three years, and then only very occasionally since.

She glanced up at Nick, and he was studying her thoughtfully, his eyes concerned.

'I'm sorry,' he murmured. 'That must have been horrible.'

She swallowed. 'It's fine. I'm over it,' she said, not quite truthfully. 'And I'm a grown-up. I have my own home now, and even if it's inadequate in many ways it's still mine, my sanctuary, the place I can relax and be myself, and it might not be perfect, it might not be immaculate or particularly restful, but it's still home, or the closest thing we have to one, and in the grand scheme of things we're really very lucky. We could be a great deal worse off.'

Maisie pushed her bowl away and looked across at them.

'Mummy, can we go in the garden?'

'That's up to Nick. He might be busy—'

'No, you're fine,' he said, and before she could say any more, he slid open the door in the hall and let them out.

They stayed for an hour, the two older children exploring every inch of the garden with

Rufus running around with them and wagging his tail furiously while he and Ellie sat on a bench with Evie close by and kept an eye on them, and then she took them away and he watched them go with mixed feelings.

They were lovely kids, but like all small people they were a challenge, and she was right, he did have things he should be doing. Things like sorting through the boxes in the first bedroom—although maybe not today.

Instead he gravitated back to the kitchen, staring out of the window and trying to process what she'd said about her mother, and her father's new wife.

How had it felt, going back to her home and finding all trace of her mother had been eradicated from it by her replacement? Dreadful, even if it had been four years later. And although she'd said she was over it, he didn't believe it, not in the slightest bit. Losing her mother at fifteen must have been devastating for her, and he thought back to her words on—when? Monday?—when he'd asked after the widow of her patient who'd died.

*You know how it is. Even when you know it's coming, it's always so final, and we're never ready for that.*

He'd thought she was talking professionally, but she hadn't been, of course. She'd been talking about the loss of her mother.

Poor Ellie. And her words about her house, or at least her home, being her sanctuary. He could understand that, too, because he'd lost his home when he and Rachel had split up and he'd moved back home to help his parents with his dying brother, and although this house wasn't yet as he wanted it, it was definitely his home, his sanctuary, the place he could go and be himself, to borrow her words.

Although at least he liked his house. He got the distinct feeling she didn't like hers at all, but maybe he'd misunderstood because she'd certainly described it as home.

Home is where the heart is?

Not that she'd said that, not in so many words, but it was where she was bringing up her family and, with the possible exception of Maisie, it was the only home they'd ever known.

He poured himself another coffee and sat down at the kitchen table with the last of the crisps and watched Rufus, who was sitting at attention by the front door and looking hopeful.

'Rufus, they've gone, go and lie down, mate,' he said gently, but Rufus didn't move, and every now and then he gave a little whine.

He knew just how the dog felt. Even though he'd wanted to be alone with his thoughts, suddenly he didn't, and the house seemed huge and empty and soulless without them all.

Although that was what he wanted, wasn't it? To be alone? But perhaps not quite this much. Not that he wanted the children, lovely though they were. He didn't need that in his life, didn't want any more responsibility or involvement, didn't need anyone else depending on him or coming to rely on him in any way. He was done with that.

But Ellie—Ellie was a different matter altogether. She didn't want that sort of relationship from him either, and this time next week the children would be with their father and he'd have her to himself again. He could hardly wait.

He pulled out his phone and started looking for things that they could do, and then gave up, because he realised it didn't matter what they did as long as they were together. Maybe a stroll around the town, to help him get to know it, or a trip across the river on the ferry—whatever. He didn't care. He just wanted to be with her.

And if he had a grain of sense or any instinct of self-preservation, he'd be worried about that, but he wasn't, because he was having way too much fun and it had been a long time coming. This was his time, and he was going to enjoy it if it killed him.

# CHAPTER SIX

THE WEEK CRAWLED BY, but finally it was Friday and she dropped the children's bags off with Liz and Steven, took the children to nursery and bounced into the staff room with a smile.

'Someone's happy,' Dev said with a grin, and she beamed at him.

'Because it's the weekend, and David has the children, so I'm going to crawl into bed when I get home and stay there until Sunday,' she said blithely. Well, it wasn't a lie—

'Sounds like an excellent plan. I might do that myself.'

Nick's voice came from over her shoulder, and she felt a startled laugh bubble up and caught it just in time.

'Coffee?' he asked her, walking over to the kettle, his face deadpan, and she couldn't look at him because she just *knew* his eyes would finish her off.

'Um—thanks. That would be lovely,' she

mumbled, and sat down at the table, pretending interest in her phone. He put her mug down in front of her with a decisive plonk and she looked up and met his mischievous eyes and nearly lost it. 'Thank you,' she croaked, and he just gave her a wicked grin.

'My pleasure,' he murmured innocently, and walked out, leaving her to gather herself together in peace. She gave him two minutes to get out of the corridor, then put her phone away, picked up her coffee and went down to her consulting room. Instantly there was a tap on the door, and she opened it to find him there.

'What can I do for you?' she said with a smile, and his mouth twitched.

'Well, there's an interesting question,' he said, so softly she could hardly hear it, and he propelled her gently back into the room, pushed the door shut with his foot and kissed her thoroughly.

She pulled away with a laugh. 'Stop it! I have to concentrate.'

'Well, so do I, but you just blew that out of the water by announcing your weekend plans,' he said with a grin. 'I was going to do an internet order, assuming those plans include me?'

'Absolutely! Well, unless you don't—'

'Oh, I do. I definitely do. So, any special requests?'

'Whatever. I'll try anything.'

His mouth kicked up at the side. 'I've found that out already. I was talking about food.'

She bit her lip and pushed him towards the door, trying hard not to laugh. 'Go away, Nick. I've got twenty patients to see this morning, a lot of admin to get through and a chronic conditions clinic before I can go home. Order whatever you want. When do you finish?

'Six thirty, if I'm lucky.'

She nodded. 'Call me when you're done, and I'll walk round. I don't want David seeing my car on your drive.'

'Is he likely to?'

'Maybe. They'll walk that way to the beach if the weather's nice enough to play on the sand. I hope they don't, because they'll tell him all about going to your house if they walk past it.'

He cocked his head on one side and frowned a little. 'Would that matter? Is that really such an issue?'

She nodded, not sure why it was but just feeling uneasy about it. 'Yes. I think it would. I don't really want him to know about us. I don't want him speculating, or asking me questions, or interrogating the children. It's none of his business what I do.'

'Would he, though? Interrogate them?'

'I don't know. Possibly. It's just—I want this for us, Nick. I don't want to share it. It feels too private.' Too new, if she was honest, although she wasn't saying that to him, but she could see from his eyes that he understood.

'Yeah, you're right, and it's not far—and you won't need much luggage, not if you get your way,' he added, and he gave her a smiling peck on the lips and let himself out, leaving her to ponder on exactly why it was she didn't want David to know.

Because it was none of his business?

Or because the way Nick made her feel was so unlike her, so alien to the person she'd thought she was, that she didn't dare to believe in it?

After all, what did they have, apart from a shared interest in medicine, and hot sex? Very hot sex, hot enough to melt the paint, a side of herself she'd never known existed—but what kind of a basis was that for a relationship?

That wasn't all they had, though. There was also tenderness, on both sides, and respect, and something that seemed very like affection. Not love. Not yet. But…maybe?

No, she definitely wasn't ready to go public, least of all to her ex-husband and probably not even to Nick, not about that, because there were still three very important little reasons why this wasn't going anywhere. Except his bed...

She turned on her computer, dragged her mind back to business and buzzed in her first patient.

He called at a quarter to seven to say he was home, and she set off on foot with a change of clothes and her toothbrush tucked into her bag. The door swung open as she reached for the bell, and Rufus ran to her, tail wagging furiously, tongue lolling.

'Hello, poppet,' she murmured, giving him a little stroke. 'Are you pleased to see me, by any chance?'

She straightened up, and Nick drew her in with a warm and welcoming smile and closed the door behind her.

'OK?'

'I am now,' she said, smiling up at him, and he laughed softly, slid his arms round her and hugged her.

She rested her head on his chest and breathed in the scent of him, and felt peace steal over her. Such a simple thing, a hug, but there was no one in her life now to do it apart from the children, and although she cherished their hugs, Nick's warm, solid, affectionate embrace gave her a curious feeling of emotional security that had been missing for at least two years, or maybe even longer.

Maybe since she'd lost her mother twenty years ago.

No. She was being silly and sentimental. It was nothing like that.

She tilted her head back and his mouth found hers in a searching kiss that was filled with promise, but it was rudely interrupted by the sound of a car pulling up outside.

'Ah. I forgot about that. I hope you're hungry,' he said as he lifted his head, and she smiled rucfully.

'Ravenous, actually. I didn't get my lunch again. Is that your delivery?'

'No. The internet order won't be here until tomorrow because all the slots were gone, so I ordered a Chinese takeaway. I hope that's OK?'

She grinned. 'Absolutely. Bring it on!'


After they'd finished, Nick took Rufus for a walk and she tidied up in the kitchen, wiped the table, loaded the dishwasher and put it on, then filled the kettle in case he wanted coffee. He probably would, so she found clean mugs and the cafetière and put them by the kettle. It gave her a weird feeling, a sensation of unreality, as if she was caught up in some cosily domestic little bubble that was all make-believe.

What was she doing? It didn't seem real, and yet here she was...

The front door opened and Rufus came in, wagging his tail, and she put away her odd thoughts and busied herself with the kettle.

'Wine or coffee?' she asked over her shoulder, and Nick slid his arms around her from behind and nuzzled her neck, making her fizz all over at his touch.

'That would be lovely,' he murmured against her skin, and she tilted her head out of the way to give him better access.

'So which do you want?' she asked, a touch breathlessly.

'You,' he murmured, and nipped her skin gently, then straightened up. 'Failing that, wine, but we should probably let our food slide down a bit and keep the dog company for a while. He's been alone all day and it would be mean to sneak off to bed and leave him just yet, tempting though it is.'

She turned and looked up at him, wanting him even more for the fact that he'd put the dog first. That would never have occurred to David.

'You're an utter softy, do you know that?' she murmured with a smile, and looked down at the dog. 'Come on, then, Rufus. Let's go and have a snuggle on the sofa before I steal your master.'

'Sounds like an excellent plan,' Nick said, and they headed up to the sitting room. He turned on some music, settled down next to her with his arm along the back of the sofa and handed her a glass of wine.

'Oh, this is nice,' she said, resting her head back against his arm.

'The music or the wine?'

'All of it. Everything. It just doesn't feel quite real.' She turned and looked up at him, and he dropped a tender kiss on her lips and rested his head against hers.

'It's real, Ellie.'

'Is it? It doesn't feel it. I feel a bit like Alice in Wonderland, you know? I'm just waiting for someone to chop off my head.'

He chuckled, the huff of his breath teasing her cheek, and his arm hugged her closer. 'Nobody's going to chop off your head. You're safe with me.'

Was she? She wasn't at all sure about that, but one thing she did know, she didn't want to be anywhere else.

She rested her head against his and let the

music wash over her, carrying her niggling worries away.

Bliss...

She woke up with a stiff neck, the snoring dog on her lap and Nick's arm draped heavily around her shoulders.

'Hey,' she said, and poked him gently in the ribs, and his eyes fluttered open and he smiled down at her, yawned hugely and stretched, then glanced at his watch.

'It's eleven o'clock. How did that happen?' he asked, looking confused, and she chuckled.

'Search me, I've been asleep, too.'

He yawned again, and Rufus lifted his head and yawned, too, then shut his eyes and settled down again with a sigh.

'I think that's our cue to go to bed,' he said with a chuckle, and he lifted the little dog off her lap and put him on the floor, pulled her to her feet and headed down to the hall. 'I'll take him out for a quick wander, if you want the bathroom first?'

She was in bed waiting for him when he'd settled Rufus, and he bent over and dropped a kiss on her lips.

'Give me two minutes, I need a shower.'

It was nearer three, but when he got into

bed and his body came into contact with hers he let out a long, slow groan.

'Oh, that feels so good…'

'You're damp,' she murmured, and he could feel her smile against his mouth.

'Mmm. Sorry. I didn't want to keep you waiting any longer.'

She gave a soft chuckle, her breath cooling his damp shoulder as she wriggled closer. 'I'm not complaining. You smell gorgeous. I love your shower gel.'

She propped herself up on one elbow and traced her finger over his chest, blowing on his nipples and teasing them with her fingertip before running it down over his ribs and sliding the flat of her hand over his hip.

He reached for her, but she pushed his arms out of the way and straddled him, and he sucked in his breath and met her eyes in the soft lamplight as she rocked gently against him, a naughty smile flickering around her soft, full mouth.

'You're evil, do you know that?' he growled through gritted teeth, and her smile widened.

'Mmm. Fun, isn't it?'

'It's torture,' he corrected, and groaned as she rocked her hips again.

'Want me to put you out of your misery?'

He let out a soft huff of what started as

laughter and ended as a gasp, and the chuckle echoed through her body straight into his.

'Ellie...'

She lifted up a fraction, and he closed his eyes and reached for her, but she batted him away again, pinning his arms down above his head.

'Stay there,' she told him, and he stayed, although it almost killed him, while she teased and tormented him until he was ready to howl with frustration.

And then she lowered herself down onto him slowly, taking him into her body inch by torturous inch.

He nearly lost it, and he gripped her hips and held her still, his eyes closed, not daring to look at her until the moment passed, but then he tilted his hips and she gasped, and he opened his eyes and watched her as she rose and fell in a slow, steady rhythm that threatened to kill him.

God, she was beautiful, her body strong and yet soft, full and lush and, oh, so tempting. He wanted to roll her over and drive into her, but she'd threaded her fingers through his and was pinning his hands above his head, holding him down.

He could so easily have overwhelmed her,

but he didn't want to. He just wanted her in reach, and right now she wasn't.

He stretched his arms out to the side, her fingers still locked with his, and it brought her breasts into reach. 'That's better,' he muttered, and he lifted his head and drew a nipple into his mouth, making her whimper. She let him go then, sitting up a little and gripping his shoulders, and he reached up and cupped the weight of her breasts in his palms, feeling the soft fullness of them fill his hands.

'You're so lovely,' he murmured. 'Come here. I need to kiss you and you're too far away.'

She smiled and lowered her head, her mouth finding his in a sweet, tender kiss that blew him away because it was so unexpected, so gentle, so filled with warmth and emotion as well as sensual promise.

He cradled her head in his hands and kissed her back, and the sensation spiralled as she rocked harder against him and shattered his self-control.

Done with patience, he held her tightly and rolled them over, their bodies locked together, his mouth still on hers but urgent now, too close for subtlety, too needy to wait.

'Come with me,' he growled raggedly, and he felt her body tighten, her hands clawing at him, her breath locked in her throat. And then she bucked against him, sobbing, her body contracting around him, and they tumbled together headlong into oblivion.

They didn't spend the entire weekend in bed, mostly because of Rufus but also because the weather was gorgeous and they wanted to get out into the fresh spring air.

'I don't know the area. Where would you like to go?' he asked, and she replied without hesitation.

'Can we go to Walberswick? I loved it when we went there last summer. Maisie and Oscar pottered about on the sand for ages, and I sat with Evie on my lap and tried to stop her eating sand. Rufus would love it, and it's beautiful. Fabulous sandy beach, sea stretching out to the horizon in front of you, sand dunes behind you—just lovely. It was a bit of a trek, though, and Oscar got carsick, so we haven't been since, but I'd love to go again.'

'We'll do that, then,' he said with a smile, and they drove up the coast to Walberswick, parked the car and made their way to the beach.

'Wow, it's lovely,' he said as the vista opened up in front of them, and they headed through the dunes and down to the sand.

The tide was almost out, the sand damp and firm underfoot, so they took off their shoes, rolled up their jeans and strolled along hand in hand while Rufus tore in and out of the gently lapping waves and had a wonderful time.

Then the tide turned and they headed back from the beach and found a pub serving food outside, then after lunch they drove back to his house, went to bed and made love again.

There was no urgency. They took their time, exploring each other slowly and lazily until the end, and then when it was over curling up together for a nap before pulling on their clothes and heading to the kitchen.

'Crayfish and linguine with a touch of chilli?' he said, his head in the fridge.

'Ooh, that sounds nice,' she murmured, peering over his shoulder. 'And we can have the leftovers from last night as a midnight feast later.'

He straightened up and turned to look at her. 'Are you planning on working up an appetite?' he asked, his eyes speaking volumes, and she bit her lips and tried not to smile.

'Might be.'

He laughed softly, shook his head and turned back to the fridge.

'Anything I can do?' she asked, but he shook his head again and said no, and she settled down at the little breakfast bar and watched him as he worked.

'You would have been a good surgeon.'

'Nah. I can't stand for hours, my ankle doesn't like it. That was another reason for going into general practice, and then I found I liked it better, anyway. How about you? Why are you a GP?'

'Work/life balance,' she said without hesitation. 'That was why I chose it. I loved hospital medicine, but it wasn't practical if I wanted to be a mother, so I trained as a GP and discovered a whole new world, and I can't imagine doing anything else now. I love it. Love the continuity, the ability to see a patient through a course of treatment and watch them improve, be there for them if it all goes wrong and there's nothing more we can do, watching babies turn into children with distinct personalities—it's great. So varied, so interesting, so full of human emotion and—I don't know. I just feel I can really make a difference to people's lives, and that's important to me.'

He nodded thoughtfully, and flashed her a little smile.

'Exactly,' he said, the single word carrying a wealth of meaning, and then went back to preparing their meal while she watched him and wondered if she was falling in love.

No. She couldn't be. She just liked him, and they had a lot in common. That was all. It wasn't love.

Was it?

'Hi, Liz,' she said, expecting to be told when her mother-in-law was going to return the children, but then she felt a chill run over her as Liz spoke, her voice urgent.

'Ellie, can you come? Steven's had a fall and I'm going to have to take him to hospital. I think he's broken his arm—it's all right, darlings, Mummy's coming soon. Ellie, please...'

'Of course. I'm on my way. Are you at home?'

'Yes—yes, we are. Please be quick.'

Liz hung up, and she turned to Nick.

'My father-in-law's had a fall and Liz thinks he's broken his arm and she needs to take him to hospital. I've got to go.'

'I'll drive you home, you'll need your car,' he said without hesitation, and then as they pulled up outside he put a hand on her arm. 'Do you want me to come? I know you wanted to keep us all separate, but this is an emergency and he's bound to be in pain. I can have a look at him, maybe immobilise it, give him some pain relief. Then you can get the children out of the way so they're not distressed by it.'

She dithered for a moment, then nodded. 'If you could.'

'Of course. I'll follow you. I've got my bag in the car.'

It was a Colles' fracture. He could tell that much as he got out of the car, and he could see at a glance that it was going to need surgery.

Ellie was busy comforting Evie, who was crying in Liz's arms, and Oscar and Maisie were sitting on the edge of the drive looking a little shocked.

'Take them home, I'll deal with this,' he said gently, and she nodded, put them in the car, collected their bags from the hall and left him to sort it out, so he headed over to the man sitting on the front step, guarding his arm.

He crouched down and smiled at him, noticing that he was pale and sweaty and clearly in shock.

'Hi. Steven, isn't it? I'm Nick Cooper, I'm a new colleague of Ellie's. She asked me if I could come and lend a hand. Do you mind if I have a look?'

'No, that's fine,' he said, but he was very reluctant to move his fingers, and the fracture was clearly displaced.

'Can you feel your fingers?' he asked, touching them gently in turn.

'Yes, but they feel weird. It's broken, isn't it?' Steven said, and he nodded.

'Yes. Yes, it's definitely broken, and you'll have to go to hospital. I think you could do with an ambulance, or at least a paramedic with a decent sling before we try and move you. I'll give them a call—unless you've already done it?' he asked Liz, but she shook her head.

'No. No, I just rang Ellie and sat with them. I thought she might be able to help me get him in the car. Thank you so much for coming. It's such a help. The little ones were getting upset—'

She bit her lip and turned away, and he laid a hand on her arm and squeezed it gently.

'It's OK, I'll call an ambulance.' He pulled out his phone, passed on the information and crouched down again.

'Steven, can you remember how you fell?'

'Oh—no, not really. I was feeling a bit odd—hot, sweaty—and then I was on the floor and my arm was killing me. No idea how I got here.'

'Mmm. Sounds like you might have had a little blackout. Have you ever fainted before, or felt as if you might?'

'Not exactly, but I've felt close to it once or twice.'

'Recently?'

He nodded. 'Yes, I—I've been feeling a bit weird, but I didn't think it was anything to worry about.'

'I can't believe that!' Liz said, sitting down abruptly beside him on the step. 'What were you thinking, not telling me? Is that why you haven't wanted to drive?'

He let out a little sigh and nodded. 'I didn't want to make a fuss.'

Nick grunted. Jim Golding had been the last person to tell him that and he'd died a couple of minutes later. He gave Steven a firm look.

'You need to make a fuss when things don't feel right. I'm not saying there's necessarily anything drastic wrong, but it's really important that you get things like that investigated, because falls are dangerous and they don't tend to happen spontaneously. Let me get my bag and have a listen to your chest, and then I'll give you some pain relief while we wait for the ambulance.'

His heart sounded steady, if a little fast, so Nick drew up ten mg of morphine and delivered it slowly over five minutes into a vein in his other arm. By the time he'd done that the ambulance had arrived, so he ignored his ringing phone for the third time in as many minutes and turned his attention to the crew.

'We were just round the corner having an ice cream and thinking it was a bit too quiet,' the paramedic said cheerfully, so Nick introduced himself, gave him the details of what he'd found and the drugs he'd given, handed over his patient, made sure Liz was OK, got back in his car and pulled out his phone.

Four missed calls now. She must be worrying. He'd go round to hers and put her out of her misery.

What on earth was going on?

The moment she opened the door she could hear running water, and as she stepped into the hall and felt the carpet squelch under her shoes, the sinking feeling in her stomach got a whole lot worse.

The dishwasher. She'd put it on as they'd left the house on Friday morning, and it must be leaking. Damn.

'Stay here,' she told the children, sitting them on the stairs, and she opened the kitchen door and gasped at the devastation.

Part of the ceiling was down, water streaming steadily through the joists from upstairs and splashing on the ruined kitchen units, and the light fitting was dangling at a crazy angle. Starting to panic, she ran up and opened the door of Maisie and Oscar's bedroom and found a repeat of the scene downstairs.

Sagging plasterboard, loft insulation hanging down and funnelling water straight onto a huge slab of sodden plasterboard on Maisie's bed—and above, in the loft, she could see the underside of the water tank.

Why was it leaking? How?

And she didn't even have a loft ladder so she couldn't get up there to see what was happening. Not that she'd know what to look for.

She stared around in disbelief, totally overwhelmed by the level of damage, paralysed by the shock.

*What do I do? The children. Get the children out...*

She ran back down to the children, scooped up Evie, grabbed Oscar's hand and towed him down the hall, Maisie on her heels, and as she opened the front door she heard a crash and a shudder ran through her. Another ceiling somewhere?

She ushered them out of the door before anything else happened, and rang Nick. He didn't answer, not then and not the next three times she phoned him, and then reaction set in and she started to shake.

*What if it had happened while the children*

*were asleep? They could have been killed in their beds!*

She had to take them somewhere else— somewhere safe, but where? She couldn't go back to Liz and Steven's, because they wouldn't be there, but she could go to Lucy and Andy. At least there they'd be safe. Except they were away for the weekend and might not be back yet.

*Nick, where are you? I need you...*

She put them in the car out of harm's way and was about to call him again when his car pulled onto the drive.

She'd never been so glad to see anyone in her life.

# CHAPTER SEVEN

SHE LOOKED AWFUL.

Damn. He should have called her back. He might have realised she'd be worried. He got out of his car and strode towards her.

'Hey, Ellie, he's OK—'

She shook her head. 'No. No, it's not Steven,' she said, her voice sounding really weird, and the bottom dropped out of his stomach.

'Ellie? What on earth's happened?' he said, and she fell into his arms and burst into tears. He gathered her up against his chest and held her tight, swamped with guilt for ignoring her calls. What if something dreadful had happened?

'Ellie, talk to me. What is it? Is it one of the children? What's wrong?'

She shook her head. 'No. It's my house. There's a leak—there's water everywhere and everything's ruined...'

He looked past her, past the children sitting in the car, on through the open door, but he couldn't see anything. He gave her another quick hug, let her go and put his head inside, and he could hear water running still. Not a good sign.

'Any idea where it's leaking?'

She nodded. 'The tank in the loft. At least, that's where the ceiling's down, under the tank. I've never been in there but I imagine that's what's leaking.'

'Where's your stopcock?'

'Um—under the sink, but the kitchen's trashed, so's their bedroom, and the water's running off the wires, too. I just had to get them out—'

Her face crumpled again, and he reached out and rubbed her arm gently. 'Of course you did. Stay here, I'll make sure it's safe. Where's the mains switch for the electricity?'

'Under-stairs cupboard, right in front of you.'

'OK. Back in a minute.'

She nodded, and he went in and glanced through the kitchen door and winced. She was right, it was trashed, but he wasn't going in there until he'd checked the power was off because the water was streaming down the dangling cable of the light fitting and the floor was awash, but at least the ceiling was already down and nothing else was going to happen.

He found the electricity supply under the stairs and discovered it had already tripped out, so at least it was safe and she hadn't been in any danger. Good. He turned off the mains switch and picked his way through the sodden plasterboard, turned off the stopcock under the sink and listened.

The trickle of water slowed to a steady drip. Good. That was that solved. Now for the cause. He went upstairs, squelched across the landing and looked in the bedroom above the kitchen.

Poor Ellie. No wonder she was in bits. He could hardly see the beds for the sodden plasterboard, the wet loft insulation hanging from the rafters had water dripping steadily off it, and he could see the tank through the gaping hole. Almost definitely the culprit.

He went back to the landing and looked up at the loft hatch. It wasn't hinged, which meant it wouldn't have a ladder. Great. It just got better. He dragged a chair out of her bedroom, stood on it and stretched up, tipping the hatch cover out of the way, then hauled himself up and made his way across the loft using his phone as a torch.

As he'd suspected, the float had sheared off

the arm so there'd been nothing to stop the cold tank endlessly filling, but the overflow which should have stopped the flood was still submerged, so it must be blocked. Spiders' webs? Very likely. It had happened in his parents' house, although they'd found it before it could do any harm.

Unlike Ellie. Her house was going to be out of action for weeks, maybe months. They'd be homeless.

Except they wouldn't, he realised, the inevitability of it settling in him like a familiar weight. He couldn't allow that.

He found a bit of wood lying around and wedged the arm up in case the stopcock leaked, then lowered himself down and went back to her.

She was sitting in the car with the children, and she turned her face up to him, her eyes red-rimmed but dry now.

'Well?'

'It was the tank overfilling, and the overflow must be blocked. I've turned off the water, wedged up the arm so it can't refill the tank, and the power's off so it's safe to go in, so you'd better go and find what you need for the night. You're coming back to mine.'

'Yours?'

'Well, there's no way you can stay here,

not without power or water. It isn't practical. You've got no beds for the children, no kitchen, no bathroom facilities you can use—nothing.'

She stared at him blankly. 'Nor have you—well, not beds, anyway. Um—I'll try Lucy, see if she's back—'

'No, you won't,' he said firmly. 'And before you say it, you can't go to Liz, she's got enough on her plate with Steven. And I have got beds. You're coming back to mine.'

She shook her head. 'But—we can't! You don't want us all there!'

'Don't be ridiculous, Ellie, of course I want you! And I've got three spare bedrooms. Why on earth not use them?'

She kept staring, searching his eyes, and then finally her shoulders drooped and she nodded. 'OK, if you're sure—but just for to-night, and I'll sort something out tomorrow. And I don't need to go back in. They've got overnight things in my car.'

'And you? What about yours?'

'I hadn't packed when Liz rang. I didn't have time to think about it.'

He nodded. 'OK. Well, lock it up and we'll sort it out in the morning.'

'How? We're at work.'

Her eyes were desperate, the situation overwhelming her again, so he took charge, took the responsibility off her shoulders without even thinking because that was what he did, what he'd always done all his life.

'You're not,' he said firmly. 'Not now. You need to deal with this, Ellie. I'll cover you.'

'How? We're all stretched. I'll have to work. I'll make a few calls in between. I'll be fine—'

'Don't think about it now,' he said, quietly but firmly. 'Come on, let's get you back to my house and settled in, find the children something to eat and then we can talk about it. OK?'

She nodded, to his relief, and he leant in and smiled at the children. 'Hey, guess what? You're all going to come back to my house for a sleepover. That'll be fun, won't it? Do you remember coming to my house?'

They nodded, their little faces brightening.

'Is Rufus there?' Maisie asked, and he grinned.

'Yeah, and he'll be really pleased to see you all. Come on, then. Let's go!'

It was still warm enough to be outside, the late afternoon sun slanting down into his garden, but Ellie felt chilled to the bone. She sat huddled on a bench while the children played on the grass with the delighted dog, seemingly oblivious to the turmoil going on inside her.

Not that she minded that at all. She'd rather they had no idea, because the more she thought about it, the worse their situation got.

She hugged her arms around herself and shuddered. She had no idea where Nick was or what he was doing. He'd sent them all out here into the garden, and gone back inside. Sorting out beds?

There was a double in the room next to him in a jumble of other furniture, she knew that, and a pile of bed bits and two single mattresses in the next room, but the first of the bedrooms had all the boxes stacked in it and there was no way he could deal with those in a hurry. No matter. They could share one room, if necessary. They'd be fine. At least they'd be dry and safe.

She glanced at the bedroom windows but she couldn't see any sign of movement. What was he doing?

She could always go and investigate, but she couldn't let the children out of her sight, so she stayed there, hugging her arms and wondering if it was her punishment for spending the weekend with him instead of at home.

So much for her happy little bubble.

* * *

She was still shaking.

He'd seen her through the bedroom windows, and she'd looked cold and confused and—well, devastated wasn't too strong a word.

He gave the last duvet a tug, went into the kitchen and made her a hot drink and took it outside.

'Here,' he said softly. He perched beside her on the bench at a discreet distance and put the mug in her hands, and she wrapped her fingers round it and breathed in the steam. 'Is it tea?' she asked, her voice sounding far-away and worryingly unlike her.

'Yes. Here. I've brought you chocolate.'

He held it out, and she gave him a sideways look. 'Are you giving me first aid, by any chance?' she asked with a wry smile, and he smiled back.

'Rumbled. But you're in shock, Ellie,' he said gently. 'It's a lot to take in, but you don't need to worry about tonight, at least. I've made the beds. I thought you'd want Evie in with you, so I've pushed the double bed up against the wall so she can't fall out that side, and I've built the twin beds in the other bedroom for Maisie and Oscar, so they'll be together.'

'How have you even *got* so many beds?' she asked, totally unexpectedly, and he had to hide the smile.

'I told you. I have sisters with children. We had the beds in our house in Bath so I just brought them with me.' He waved the chocolate under her nose. 'Here. Eat it.'

She glanced down, then took it from him and ate it, her eyes on the children again as if she was checking to make sure they were still safe.

'They're OK, Ellie,' he said softly. 'Nothing happened to them.'

'But it might have done. If that ceiling had come down while they were sleeping—'

'But it didn't. Nobody was there, nobody was hurt.'

'That was just sheer luck. Nick, how am I going to clean it all up? How can I get the water out of the carpets? And I'll never get that filth out of their bedding—and the kitchen! All the things on the side—the kettle, the toaster, all the storage jars...'

He could almost hear her mind working, cataloguing the extent of the disaster, and as it sank in she turned her head and looked up at him, her eyes lost.

'Nick, what do I do now? Everything's

going to need replacing—where on earth do I start?'

To hell with the discreet distance. He shifted closer, put his arm around her shoulders and hugged her up against his side. 'You contact the insurance company in the morning, you tell them what's happened, and you hand it over to them. You do have insurance, I take it?'

'Of course I do, but what will they do? Get a plumber, I suppose, and then what?'

'They'll clear the house of anything that's been damaged, put in dehumidifiers to dry out the structure and once it's all dry they'll repair it, redecorate and re-carpet it, replace the damaged furniture and light fittings, maybe refit the kitchen—'

'But...that'll take weeks!'

'It will. It'll be several weeks, maybe even months, but that's fine. You're all safe, you've got somewhere to live—don't worry. It'll all work out, Ellie.'

She shook her head and eased away from him, her face looking stunned as the enormity of it all sank in.

'We can't stay here that long. It's not fair, it's not reasonable, and it's the last thing you want.'

'No, it isn't,' he said, trying to sound convincing, but she was shaking her head again.

'Yes, it is! You told me you were ready for a quiet life. Believe me, there's nothing quiet about life with my children, and I can't live on eggshells in case they upset you—'

'Ellie, stop it,' he said gently, taking hold of her hands and stilling them before she slopped tea all over herself. 'It's fine,' he lied, as much to himself as to her. 'We'll be fine, and if you and they aren't happy here, then the insurance company will find you somewhere to go, but for now, at least, you don't need to worry. Let me do this for you, please.'

She stared at him as if he'd got two heads. 'Why? Why would you put yourself out like this?'

'Why wouldn't I? You'd do it for me, I know you would. You'd do it for anyone.' He gave a smile that felt a little crooked. 'You remember telling me why you liked general practice? Because you could make a difference to people's lives, and that's important. It's important for all of us, and it's so easy for me to do this for you, and if it makes your life easier now, then that makes me happy. And anyway, why wouldn't I want to have you around? In case you haven't noticed, I rather like your company.'

He saw something flicker in her eyes, and guessed what she was thinking before she even spoke.

'We can't...' She broke off, and he rolled his eyes and sighed, a little hurt that she could think so little of him.

'Ellie. Seriously? Your house is trashed, you and the children are homeless, and you think I'm worried about sex? I thought you were a better judge of character.'

She swallowed. 'I'm sorry. It's just—the situation's never arisen before, but I made a decision long ago that there would be nobody sharing my bed while the children were around, and certainly not a man I've only known a few weeks. Even if they have been pretty significant weeks...'

He smiled and hugged her again. 'They have, but, honestly, I'm not stupid and I'm not selfish and I absolutely understand where you're coming from. I'm offering you somewhere safe to stay, no strings, and at the moment you're all out of options.'

'We could always stay with Liz and Steven once he's out of hospital.'

'I wouldn't have thought so, or not for a while. Steven's fracture is going to need surgery, and once he comes home he'll need help with all sorts of things, so I doubt you'll even be able to rely on Liz for a while, at least for the first week or so until he's over it and on the mend. It was a nasty break.'

She nodded slowly, and swallowed. 'Yes, I saw. I was wondering about that, just before I opened my front door.' She shook her head. 'I haven't even given him a thought since, and his problems are far worse than mine. What kind of a person does that make me?'

'Worried. Worried for your home and your children and their safety and security—and anyway, you knew he was being taken care of and there was nothing you could do to change things for him, so why would you think about him when he wasn't your top priority? You've had more pressing things to deal with, and he would understand that. And anyway, he's in the right place and I'm sure he'll be OK. Apparently he fainted, so they'll probably want to check that out as well. Liz said she'd let you know as soon as she had news.'

She nodded again, and finally leant back against the bench and drank her tea, her eyes on the precious little people that were her life, and he sat with his arm behind her along the back of the bench and watched her watching over them while his heart ached for her.

He just hoped this situation didn't end up breaking any of their hearts or spoiling the fledgling relationship he had with Ellie, but that was the least of his worries, because it wasn't just about how he felt, or her, come to that, it was about the children.

And they, he reminded himself, were all that really mattered.

Her phone rang just as the children were sitting down to eat, and she pulled it out and sighed.

'Sorry, I have to get this, it's David,' she said, and walked into the kitchen.

He could hear snatches of what she was saying, giving him the gist of what had happened. Then he heard his name, and his ears pricked up. Whatever happened to keeping it secret? And what would David be making of it? Not that there was any way they could keep it from him. The children were bound to let it out.

'Hey, Oscar, don't feed Rufus,' he said softly, dragging himself back to the task in hand. 'People's food isn't good for dogs.'

'Why?'

He stifled the smile. His sisters' endless choruses of 'why?' had driven him nuts when they were this age, and his nephews and nieces had carried on the tradition. Apparently it was universal.

'It just isn't. Their tummies are different,'

he explained, and waited for the inevitable re-action.

'Why?'

'They just are,' he said, and steered the conversation away from the dog's digestion. 'He had fun with you in the garden.'

'I like him,' Maisie said. 'He always looks happy.'

'He is happy when you're here. He loves children. Have you all finished?'

Oscar pushed his plate away and looked hopeful. 'Can we have pudding?'

He scanned the fridge in his head. 'Would you like some yogurt?'

'Do you have ice cream?'

'No, Maisie, I don't, I'm afraid. I've got yogurt and blueberries, and I can cut up some banana. How about that?'

It seemed to appeal, so he cleared the plates and took the fruit and yogurt back to the table, giving Ellie a reassuring wink in passing.

She flashed him a smile, hung up a few moments later and followed him back.

'Sorry about that. He'd had a message from his mother but he couldn't get hold of her and he wanted to know what was going on.'

He sliced banana into the bowls and glanced at her. 'Is he coming back?'

She shook her head. 'No. He can't, he's at the airport. I've said I'll deal with it.'

'Did you tell him about the house?' he asked, dolloping yogurt on the fruit.

'Yes, and I told him we were staying with a friend so he didn't need to worry, but he wasn't, really, he was more worried about his father. He knew you'd helped Steven, and he seemed to know who you were. Guys, did you and Daddy walk past the house this weekend on your way to the beach, and did you tell him all about Nick and Rufus?'

They nodded, and she exchanged a speaking glance with him before looking back at the children. 'I think you need help with that, Evie,' she said, and took the baby's spoon out of her hand, and he watched her feed the little one and wondered what else had been said.

It was another hour before the children were tucked up in bed, and half an hour after that before they were asleep. Even so, she sat for a good while longer on the double bed she'd be sharing with Evie, until she heard the soft sound of Nick's bare feet padding down the hall.

He paused at the door and raised an eyebrow in enquiry.

'OK?' he mouthed, and she nodded and

got carefully off the bed, put the pillows in the way so Evie couldn't roll out and tiptoed across the room.

'What's wrong?' she asked in a quiet undertone.

'Nothing. It's just you've been ages, and I wondered if you were having difficulty settling them.'

She shook her head. 'No. I'm just worried they'll wake up, and it's a long way to the sitting room. I don't think I can leave them. They might wake up and not know where they are.'

'Fancy a coffee?'

She sighed with joy, and smiled at him. 'I'd *love* a coffee. I'll come with you and get it and bring it back here.'

He shook his head. 'I have a better idea. Go into my bedroom, and I'll bring it. We can sit on the bed and talk with the door open, and you'll hear if any of them stir.'

She hesitated, and he shook his head slowly and gave her a rueful smile. 'Ellie, I thought we'd had this conversation? Go on, go and get comfortable. I won't be long.'

She went up on tiptoe and kissed his cheek. 'You are such a star,' she murmured, and went into his bedroom to wait for him. The overhead light seemed too bright, so she put on the bedside lights and settled herself against the pillows she'd slept on only last night, wrapped in his arms.

It seemed a lifetime ago, and so much had happened in that time.

She heard his footsteps and he appeared with coffee and a heaped plate on a tray. She sat up straighter, suddenly aware that she was hungry.

'Are those sandwiches, or am I hallucinating?'

He grinned and shook his head. 'I made them a little while ago, because I wasn't sure if you'd be able to leave the children. I thought you could eat while you watch them, if necessary, but this is a much better idea.'

His smiled warmed her all the way to her toes, and she shuffled over and he settled himself beside her and handed her a mug, putting the plate down on the bed between them.

'I could get used to this,' she murmured contentedly.

'Feel free,' he said with a smile, and leant over and dropped a chaste, tender kiss on her lips. 'Now eat.'

She ate hungrily, then sat back with a sigh and sipped her coffee. 'Bliss. I was starving. Thank you so much—for everything. I don't know what we would have done without you.'

'Well, that's easy. You wouldn't have been

in this mess without me, because you would have found the leak much earlier because you wouldn't have been here.'

'I might not have done. I might not have found it until the ceiling fell down on the children in the middle of the night. It's going to give me nightmares,' she said, and suppressed a shudder.

'No, it won't,' he said firmly, 'because it didn't happen and it's all fine—well, no, not fine, obviously, but at least everyone's OK. So what did David have to say about the house?'

She sighed and rolled her eyes. 'Oh, not a lot. He wanted to know if we were all right, but he was more worried about his father, naturally, and of course he couldn't come back to see him and make sure he was all right. He asked if he could leave me to deal with it. I pointed out he usually does.'

'I heard you mention my name.'

'Yes, he brought it up because he knew you'd been there helping. He said, "Is that the Nick who lives in Jacob's Lane?" so I imagine the children will have given him chapter and verse when they walked past. They don't normally hold back. He certainly knew you'd got a dog.'

'Does he know you're staying here?'

She shook her head. 'No, and I didn't tell

him. I didn't want him jumping to conclusions. He wanted to know where I'd been, as I obviously hadn't been at home, and I just told him I was away for the weekend. I could hear the cogs turning, and I wouldn't be surprised if he puts two and two together and makes ten, but there you go, there's nothing I can do.'

'I wouldn't worry about it. You are divorced, aren't you? You're entitled to a life.'

She gave a little huff of laughter. 'Oh, yes. We're very definitely divorced, and I know he hasn't been a saint since we split up, but then it's different for him. He's not a mother.'

'It's not different!'

'It is, or sort of. He doesn't live with them, and they never see him in his other life. It's harder for me to have a relationship, and I don't know how he'd take it. Not that it's any of his business, but I'd still rather not discuss it with him. He wanted to know why we weren't going to stay with his parents. I had to point out that I don't have keys, she was at the hospital with his father, either waiting for him to go into Theatre or waiting while he was in there, and if he couldn't get hold of her then I couldn't, so how was I supposed to get the keys, and anyway she had quite enough to worry about without being bothered by my problems. I also told him not to tell her about the house, because I really don't want her worried. I'll tell her when I know Steven's OK.'

'Good plan. And in the meantime, stop worrying. It'll all sort itself out.'

She gave a short sigh. 'I don't think so. I think I'm going to have to sort it.' She dropped her head back and stared blankly at the wall opposite. 'Oh, what on earth am I going to do, Nick?' she said, feeling utterly defeated and so, so tired. 'I don't even know where to start.'

'Keep it simple. Lucy should be back by now. Phone her and tell her you need the day off tomorrow, and then call the insurance company first thing in the morning. Do you have the documents?' he asked, all practicality, but she hadn't even thought about that.

'Yes—but not on me. They're in the dining room, but at least it's dry in there so they should be OK. I can get them tomorrow.'

'I'll go and get them for you now. Where are they, exactly?'

'Oh—are you sure? You don't need to do that, Nick, I could go.'

'What, and leave the children with a virtual stranger? No. I'll go, Ellie. It's better for them, and I don't mind. So, how do I find these documents?'

She gave in, because of course he was right. 'In the dresser—far end, bottom shelf, in an expanding file full of all the important stuff. It's black, with a red handle, and my laptop's in there, too. That could be useful.'

'Anything else there that you want? Anything valuable? Bearing in mind that the alarm's not set because the power's off.'

She swallowed. 'Only my mother's jewellery.'

'Where is it?'

'In my bedroom, in the…' She gave a despairing laugh and started again, feeling colour creep into her cheeks. Ridiculous, considering what they'd done right here in this bed over the weekend. 'It's in the top right-hand drawer, under my underwear. It's at the back, under the stuff I never wear.'

'What colour is it?'

'What, my underwear, or the jewellery box?'

His mouth twitched. 'I think I pretty much know what colour your underwear is. I meant your jewellery box.'

She couldn't help smiling. 'Tan leather. It's the only thing in there apart from the undies. Actually you could bring me some clean stuff for tomorrow. That would be really nice.'

'OK. Is that all there is? Any other jewellery?'

She shook her head, fingering the ring she

wore on her wedding finger. 'Only this. It was Mum's, too.'

He reached out and laid his hand over hers, giving them a gentle squeeze. 'I'm sorry, Ellie.'

She glanced at him, puzzled. 'Why should you be sorry? You didn't flood my house.'

'No. I meant your mum,' he said softly.

She swallowed hard, suddenly swamped with emotion, and for a moment she couldn't speak. Then she sucked in a breath and met his thoughtful, troubled gaze. 'Thank you.'

She leant over and kissed him, and then smiled at him. 'David said his mother had called you a good Samaritan, and she was right, you are. I don't know what I would have done if you hadn't been around this afternoon to help with Steven and then this. I was so shocked, so scared for the kids, for what might have happened, and there you were, taking control, turning off the water, checking the electricity was off, sorting it out—if you hadn't been there...'

'But I was, and you're here now.'

'But only for one night.'

He shook his head slowly, his eyes intent and sincere. 'You don't have to go, you know. You can stay here for as long as you need to, as long as it takes.'

'Nick, it could be months, you said so yourself.'

'That's fine. Really. You're safe, the children are safe, and that's all that matters. Everything else can be dealt with, starting right now.'

He leant over and kissed her, a tender, lingering kiss, then got off the bed and walked towards the door, but she stopped him.

'Nick, wait, you need keys.'

'They're on the side in the kitchen, and don't worry, I'll make sure it's all secure before I leave. Phone Lucy,' he added, and then he went out and a few moments later she heard the front door shut and the crunch of gravel as he drove away.

She lifted her fingers to her lips, and could have cried at his thoughtfulness, his gentleness, his compassion. Instead she pulled out her phone, sucked in a deep breath and called Lucy.

Time to put on her big-girl pants.

Doing it all by torchlight didn't make things easier, but at least her directions were good.

He found the big black file and her laptop and put them in the hall, then went upstairs and looked in her underwear drawer for the jewellery box and some clean undies for her for tomorrow, but he had to struggle to keep his mind in order, especially when he found the bra he'd taken off her the first time. None of that in his immediate future, he thought with a sigh, and picked up a random selection of this and that, shut the drawer firmly and headed for the stairs.

Then he stopped and shone the torch into the ruined bedroom, and saw teddies.

Wet, soggy teddies, but much loved.

He picked his way carefully across the room, and felt the floor giving underneath his feet. The chipboard must have degraded with the wet. Well, just so long as it held his weight, but at least the carpet would stop him falling through into the kitchen. He hoped…

He tested the floor and found the position of a joist, and walked along it, grabbed the teddies off the children's sodden beds and made his way cautiously out again, went into Evie's room and picked up her teddy from her cot and went back downstairs, put everything he'd gathered together into the car and went back into the kitchen.

He'd brought his cool box, and he emptied the contents of her freezer drawers into it, decanted her fridge into carrier bags, put them in the car, and then hesitated, another thought occurring to him. They might be ruined, but on the other hand, they might not. Worth a try.

He went back into the kitchen, took the children's pictures off the fridge, put the magnets in his pocket, locked the house and drove back.

As he pulled up on the drive and got out, the front door opened. Ellie stood there, framed in the light, and for the first time since he'd moved there it truly felt like coming home.

To a family?

Not his, though, and if she had her way, never his. Not that he wanted that—did he?

# CHAPTER EIGHT

SHE'D BEEN WAITING in the kitchen for him, watching out of the window with one ear listening for the children, and as the car turned onto the drive and the lights swept across the window, she felt a little surge of—what? Relief? Joy?

She didn't wait to analyse it, just went to the door and opened it, and as he stepped inside he took her into his arms and the world seemed to right itself.

'I'm sorry I've been so long. Are you OK?'

His arms felt so good around her, and she rested her head against his chest and breathed him in. 'I am now. I'm sorry I was a bit hysterical earlier. Did you get everything?' she murmured.

'Mmm-hmm, and I brought a few other things,' he said, dropping his arms and easing back a little. 'I emptied the fridge-freezer, but mine's fairly empty so we should be OK. And

I brought their teddies from their beds, too, but they're a bit soggy and dirty. They'll need a wash, but I thought they might want them. Oh, and there's something else. I hope they're all right, but it was hard to see by torchlight.'

He went back to the car, opened the back door and took something out, and as she saw what he'd brought her hand flew up to her mouth and she let out a little sob, overwhelmed that he'd thought of something so small and yet so significant.

'You brought their pictures?'

His grin was a bit crooked. 'Yeah. It seemed a shame to leave them, and my fridge is a bit bare. I thought it might help them feel at home. Here. Stick them up.'

He pulled the fridge magnets out of his pocket, piled them on the worktop and left her to deal with them while he brought in all the other things.

'I'll need to find you room in a chest of drawers, and make sure I remember to give you a set of keys,' he said, putting the stuff down.

'We're only here for the night,' she reminded him, and he rolled his eyes, but even as she'd said it, she knew it was a token protest, and she couldn't think of anywhere she'd rather be. She just hoped he didn't regret it in the morning, but she wouldn't say anything to the children yet about how long they'd stay, just in case he changed his mind.

They sat down at the dining table after she'd unpacked everything, and while they drank another coffee and ate the cake he'd found in her fridge, she tracked down her house insurance documents in the file.

'Well, that looks pretty straightforward,' she said after a quick scan through them. 'All I have to do is ring them and they send an assessor and it all goes from there.'

'Good. And Lucy was OK?'

She nodded. 'Yes, Lucy was wonderful, and said if I need anything just ask. I'm sure there will be a million things, but they'll crop up when I know I haven't got them. Oh, and Liz phoned. Steven's out of surgery, and he's OK, but he's staying in for a few days for investigations. They think he might have some kind of heart condition that caused the blackout, so they want to look into that.'

'Yeah, they will,' Nick murmured, frowning. 'I wonder what caused it? Arrhythmia? He said he felt hot and sweaty and a bit weird, and he was very pale.'

'Who knows. I just hope it's nothing too serious. So tomorrow, Lucy said you'll split all my patients between you, and if I can get this done early I'll come in and do what I can. I'm going to take the kids to nursery but I can't ask Liz to pick them up, at least not until they know more about why Steven fell.'

'No, of course not. Don't worry about it. We'll work it all out somehow.'

'Somehow' was right.

It was chaos, the usual Monday morning rush after the weekend compounded by the fact it was the Easter holidays and Dev was off.

He and Lucy and Brian divvied up the patients between them, diverted some to the nurse practitioners and took advantage of the ones who failed to turn up for their appointments by catching up a little with the backlog, and by lunchtime they were more or less there.

For the morning lists, at least.

And then as they sat signing repeat prescriptions and checking results in the staff room, Ellie appeared looking harassed and racked with guilt.

'I'm so, so sorry. Has it been hell?' she asked, and he got to his feet and put the kettle on.

'It's been fine. We've managed. How did you get on with the insurance company?'

'That's why I'm here. The assessor's coming at two thirty, so I've asked nursery to keep the children until five. If I get away early, I'll come and do my afternoon list, or as much of it as I can, but if not I don't know what to do.'

'You don't have to do anything,' Brian said firmly. 'You don't need to be here at all today. Go and sort out your house stuff and we'll see you tomorrow if you're able to come in, and if you're not, then we won't. Now sit down and have a coffee and relax for a minute.'

'That's not fair. Have you got any results I can look at, or repeats to sign?'

'No, they're done, but you might want to look at Jim Golding's PM report,' Nick said quietly, putting a mug of coffee down beside her. 'He had an undiagnosed aneurysm in the aortic arch. It ruptured.'

She scanned it, and her eyes widened. 'Really? Wow. Poor Jim. No wonder he was feeling peaky. It must have been brewing for days—weeks, maybe.'

'Mmm. Says it was catastrophic, so the DNAR was irrelevant. We couldn't have resuscitated him anyway.'

She nodded slowly, and he met her eyes over the top of the screen. They were sad, filled with regret, and he cut her off before she could say it.

'You didn't let him down. The other thing

he said to me was, "I'm glad it's not Dr Kendal." I don't think he wanted you to be upset, and I have a feeling he knew he was going to die then. He's was ready, Ellie.'

She nodded. 'I know. He told me, when he asked for the DNAR. He said he didn't want anyone trying to save him if his time was up, because he was ready to go and join Kitty. He missed her so much—sorry...'

She swiped away a tear, and Lucy looked up and shook her head.

'There's no point at all in telling you not to get involved, is there?' she said with a wry smile, and Ellie gave an uneven little laugh.

'No, probably not. Right, I'd better go and meet my assessor and see what he makes of it.'

'Don't come back today,' Brian said firmly. 'You've had enough to deal with. We can cope.'

'But I—'

'But nothing. Look what you all did for me while I was off. What you're still doing. Go, Ellie. Do what you have to do. The world won't stop turning. It never does.'

She nodded and went, and Nick turned to him.

'Thanks. She's been so determined not to let anyone down, but—Brian, if you'd seen that house... And her father-in-law fell because he'd had a blackout, so that's now under investigation and she's bound to be worried about him, too. I think he's one of our patients.'

'He is. I'll look into it,' Brian said, and got stiffly to his feet. 'I'll be glad when the builders finish this week and we get our new staff room downstairs. My hip really doesn't like the stairs. Doesn't like anything much. I suppose I need to bite the bullet and get it done.' He gave them a crooked grin and limped out, and Nick met Lucy's eyes.

'He's needed a hip replacement for years,' she told him quietly, 'but he couldn't do it because of his wife, and since then—well, I don't think he feels he can take the time off.'

'That's crazy.'

'That's general practice, Nick. It's what it's like now. I can't tell you how glad we all are that you're here. And—Ellie. Tread carefully, Nick. She's been through a lot and this is the last thing she needed.'

'I know. Don't worry, Lucy, I'm looking after her—after all of them.'

She held his eyes. 'Don't break her heart.'

He frowned, and Lucy shook her head. 'Don't pretend you don't know what I'm talking about, Nick. I've seen the way you look at each other. I'm not stupid.'

'Nor am I, and the last thing I want is to

hurt her. I'm just offering her a roof over their heads and a safe place to be, for as long as it takes.'

'Good.' She put the signed prescription on the pile and stood up, letting the subject drop. 'Back to the grind, I suppose. Are you coming?'

He nodded and followed her, her words echoing in his head.

*Been through a lot...last thing she needed... don't break her heart...*

'How did it go?'

Ellie shrugged and tried to smile, but she knew it was a poor effort.

'OK, in a way. They'll fix everything, I just have to remove what I want to keep with me, and they'll put everything that isn't damaged in the rooms that are OK and fix the ones that are broken, then replace the damaged stuff.'

'Timeline?'

She shrugged again and put the knife down, abandoning the vegetables. 'Weeks? Maybe up to two months? The main problem is the chipboard flooring in the bedroom, and the kitchen units and worktop. It's swollen and disintegrating and it all needs to be replaced, and of course the wiring needs sorting and it'll need decorating and carpeting and—oh, it goes on and on.'

He nodded, his eyes searching hers. 'Do you get to choose the kitchen?'

'Within reason, apparently. If I want a better one I can pay the difference, and if I want to make changes to the house I can do that and pay the extra, so I could do that—put doors in between the sitting room and dining room so it's essentially one space, and refit the kitchen and reinstate the door to the garden, but...' She shrugged. 'I'm not sure. It still isn't big enough, the garden's too tiny for a proper extension, and it might make more sense to get it fixed and sell it as it is and buy something that works for us.'

He nodded, still studying her, and then he tipped his head on one side. 'You said "OK, in a way". So what's not OK?'

She gave a tiny huff of what should have been laughter if it wasn't so unfunny. 'I don't have temporary replacement accommodation insurance. It's an optional extra on that policy, and I obviously didn't tick the box.'

She swallowed, because he probably didn't want to hear the next bit, but he got in before her.

'Well, that's not an issue,' he said, before she could say the words. 'I've said you can stay here, and you can. You don't *have* to, obviously, but if you would like to, then I don't see the problem.'

She searched his eyes, and then they went all blurry and she had to blink.

'Thank you. That's very generous of you, so we will, please, for now. I'll see how Liz and Steven feel once he's better—'

'Ellie. It's fine. They're not young any more, and little children are wearing.'

'Well, then, you don't want them, either,' she said, racked with guilt again, but he shook his head.

'Nonsense. That's not what I'm saying. I just know that when my parents have one of my sisters over with their family for the weekend, by Sunday night they're exhausted and more than ready for them all to go home, much as they love having them. I would say they're pretty much the same age, both the children and the grandparents.'

'And how about you? What happens when you get sick of us and you're ready for us to go home? Because we can't, Nick, we don't have one any more—' She broke off, her voice cracking, and turned away, sucking in a deep breath and trying to get herself back under control.

She heard the soft sound of his footsteps,

felt his hands cup her shoulders and draw her gently back against his chest.

'Ellie, stop it. Stop torturing yourself. Yes, it'll get noisy and frustrating at times, and we'll trip over each other a bit, but honestly, I love having you all here and all families go through that. There are times when my sisters could cheerfully rehome their children, but it usually lasts about ten minutes. We'll cope. I'll cope. It'll be fine. Now come here and have a hug and stop worrying.'

She turned in his arms, buried her face in his shoulder and let out a ragged little sigh.

'What have I done to deserve you?' she asked, and she felt a chuckle rumble through his chest.

'You don't really know me yet. I'll probably be getting on your nerves by the end of the week.'

'Why would you do that?'

She felt his shoulders lift in a little shrug. 'As I said, you don't know me. I'm sure there are all sorts of things that'll irritate you.'

She leant back a little and looked up at him. 'Well, you haven't so far.'

He grinned. 'Give it time. Talking of which, is that our supper you're getting, or something else?'

'That's our supper. The children have been

in bed for ages, they were tired. I got the travel cot from Evie's bedroom cupboard. She didn't sleep too well last night, and nor did I with her wriggling around, so she's got her own bed now so I don't need to worry about her falling out, and I brought the baby monitor so I can relax in the sitting room without worrying, and I also brought them some toys.'

He nodded thoughtfully. 'I had an idea, I don't know if it appeals. I thought I could stack all those boxes from the other bedroom into the garage, and then you could have it as a playroom. There's a sofa bed in there, and we can turn it into a little sitting room for you.'

'We can keep out of your way, then,' she said, not sure if she felt relieved or rejected, but he just laughed.

'Ellie, that's not what I meant! But the sitting room is upstairs, and Evie could fall down them and hurt herself, which is the last thing you need. I need to get a stairgate, really, so she can't crawl up them.'

'I've got one at home. I could bring it.'

He nodded. 'Then we can keep her safe, and they can have somewhere to make a mess when they want to without you having to feel guilty—which I know you will, before you deny it. So, what's for supper?'

\* \* \*

He moved the boxes after they'd eaten.

It took him over an hour, and by the end of it his hip was aching and he was more than ready to sit down, but at least the room was clear. It just needed a vacuum while the children weren't asleep, and maybe a little table and chairs for them to sit at to draw and paint, and it would be fine.

There was nothing they could do to the carpet that would do it any harm, anyway. It was worn and tired and needed replacing, but it could wait. It could all wait, and it would have to, because Ellie and her children were his priority now, not the house.

He put the last box of Samuel's things down on the stack in the garage, and rested a hand on it, closing his eyes and breathing in slowly.

'Miss you, Sam,' he murmured, and sucking in another breath, he walked out of the garage, locked the door and headed back inside.

He could hear water running. Ellie must be in the shower, and the longing to take his clothes off and walk in there and join her was overwhelming. Hell, it was going to be tough.

He went back to the kitchen and found it was all cleared up and the dishwasher was on. He boiled the kettle, made himself a mug of tea and was about to head up to the sitting room when she appeared, wrapped in a dressing gown with a towel round her head and looking way too good for his peace of mind.

Her smile was wry. 'I don't suppose you've got a hairdryer?'

He shook his head. 'Sorry, no.'

'I need to write a list. There are loads of things I haven't got. I'll go back and get them tomorrow. And in the meantime we need to have a talk.'

He frowned at her. 'About?'

'Us being here and how we're going to manage it. If we're going to be here for weeks, we'll pay our way, obviously. A share of the electricity and gas bills, the food—all of it. Or we move,' she added as he opened his mouth, and he had a horrible feeling she meant it, so he shrugged and gave in.

'OK. I cleared the playroom.'

'I saw. Thank you so much. I'll move their toys and stuff into it tomorrow and we can keep out of your way then.'

'Ellie, you're not in my way,' he said, but she just shook her head reproachfully so he gave up.

'Whatever. Want a cup of tea?'

* * *

They fell into a sort of routine over the course of the next week.

He got breakfast for everyone on her work days, she cooked the evening meal most nights, and by the weekend she'd rounded up all the things she'd forgotten to bring from the house, and they were settling in nicely.

A bit too nicely, and she was worried that they were constantly underfoot, but when she tackled Nick about it again on Friday night he was adamant that they weren't. Nevertheless, the children spent a lot of time with him, more than was probably wise, if they weren't going to get too attached to him. And that went for her as well as the children.

'We'll keep out of your hair tomorrow,' she told him, and he rolled his eyes.

'You don't need to. I'm doing the Saturday morning surgery this weekend anyway, so I won't even be here.'

'But that's only until eleven. It's fine, they want to see their grandparents. We'll do that late morning.'

'Whatever, but you don't need to.'

'Yes, I do, Nick, because we're spending too much time together and it's going to make it difficult, especially with David.'

'How will he know?'

'Because the children will inevitably say something. All they ever talk about is you and Rufus, and while Oscar and Evie babble a lot and don't make much sense, Maisie is as clear as a bell and she's utterly besotted by you. It'll be Nick did this and Nick did that and he'll start asking awkward questions.'

His eyes went oddly blank, as if the shutters had come down. 'And that's an issue.'

'Not yet, but it could be.'

He nodded. 'OK. Well, you've got the other room now. Feel free to use it whenever you want and I'll try and keep out of your way.'

Did he sound hurt? Oh, lord, this was too difficult. Why on earth had she thought it would work?

'I didn't mean that, Nick. It's your house. We should be keeping out of your way, not the other way round.'

'Ellie, I'm done with this conversation. I know you don't want the kids getting attached to me, I get that, so I'll discourage it.' He picked up his laptop off the side and opened it at the table. 'Anyway, I've got work to do. Sorry.'

She got up from the table, clearly dismissed, and had to tell herself it was what she wanted. Wasn't it?

'That's fine. I've got a book to read. I'll see you tomorrow.'

She walked out without looking at him again, but she felt a little bit sick as she went into the playroom and closed the door, and try as she might, she couldn't concentrate on the book because the words kept blurring in front of her eyes.

Damn.

He hadn't meant to be like that, but she was right, he was spending too much time with the kids, with her, with the whole family thing, and he really hadn't expected it to be like this.

Well, he was at work in the morning, and he'd take himself and Rufus off later and go and do something else. Maybe go for a walk on the beach, but not here, because that was where they'd go, so he'd go further along towards the pier and keep out of their way.

He got out a wine glass, put it back and made some tea and took it up to the sitting room with his laptop, but he could see the light on in the playroom, and he glanced down and saw her there, her head bent over her book.

He left the lights off and stood in the shadows and watched her for a moment, then gave a sharp sigh, sat down and turned on the table lamp. He was turning into a stalker, for heaven's sake, spying on her while she read her book. And besides that, he hadn't lied, he did have work to do, things to read up on, so he made himself do it just so he didn't add lying to the list of his failings.

At ten thirty she took the children out to see their grandparents, so Nick could come back to a quiet house. They might get some sandwiches from the kiosk and eat them on the beach as it was a nice day, and if Liz didn't feel up to giving them lunch.

Obviously not, she realised as soon as Liz opened the door. She'd left the children in their car seats for a moment so she could catch up, and she was glad she had because she was shocked at how tired and strained her mother-in-law looked.

She hugged her gently. 'We won't stay long, but the children really want to see you both. Maisie's been so worried about her grandad, and they've all asked to see you. Even Evie beamed when I said your names. She tried to say Grandma, but it didn't quite work.'

'Oh, bless her. No, you must bring them in, but just for a few minutes. He's so tired.'

'I'm sure. I'm sorry I haven't been to see him but it's been—difficult,' she said vaguely, not wanting to add the burden of her house woes to Liz's already heavy load. 'So, how has he been post-op?' she asked softly.

'His arm's been very painful,' Liz said, 'and we're both a bit worried about the blackouts.'

'Has he had more?'

She sighed. 'No, but he hasn't driven for weeks, just suggested I drive if we went anywhere and I should have smelt a rat, but of course being a man he didn't do anything about it, just waited for it to go away. He didn't mention it until Nick asked him about the fall, and it's a good job he did ask or who knows when he would have bothered to mention it. Anyway, he's had a whole raft of blood tests and he was on a monitor for a while. They think he might have some kind of heart condition which causes—oh, I can't remember what they called it. Some kind of lock, and they also said something to do with dropping, but they didn't think it was that.'

'Drop attack? That's a name for a certain type of blackout but that's neurological, not cardiovascular, which would be from a heart condition. They probably said TLoC?'

'Yes, that sounds like it. So what is it? I was so tired and so worried I didn't take it all in.'

'No, I can imagine. It's short for transient loss of consciousness, which covers all sorts of reasons for fainting or losing consciousness for a brief while. It can be caused by a disruption of the heart rhythm, and it sounds like they think he might have had that. So what happens next?'

'He's going to see the cardiologist again next week, but—oh, Ellie, you know him. He hates making a fuss, and he doesn't want to go, but I'm so worried about him…'

Ellie hugged her gently. 'He must go. I'll talk to him. And don't worry, they'll sort him out. He might need a pacemaker or drugs to settle it down.'

'Oh, he's on a new drug—ami-something?'

'Amiodarone? It's an anti-arrythmic, so that makes sense. What's important is that he doesn't keep falling over, because as he's no doubt now realised, it can have consequences.' She headed back to the car. 'OK, guys, out you get, but remember, Grandad's quite sore so you need to be very quiet and gentle.'

She hoisted Evie into her arms and followed them in, and they found Steven in the sitting room, his arm propped up on a cushion, having a snooze.

He opened his eyes as they went in, and his face lit up at the sight of the children.

'Hello, my babies,' he said warmly, and Maisie wriggled up beside him and tucked herself under his good arm, and Ellie saw his eyes fill. 'Goodness, I've missed you all.'

'Are you all right, Grandad?' Maisie asked him worriedly, and he nodded and smiled down at her.

'I am now I'm having a cuddle with you.'

Oscar stood at his feet, eyeing the cast in fascination. 'What's that?' he asked, so Steven explained, and then came the inevitable, 'Why?'

'Because that's what happens when you break something. Here, why don't you play with this?' Ellie said, and handed him a car out of her bag. 'Play on the floor with Evie.'

He pulled a mulish little face. 'But I want a cuddle, too.'

'You can have a cuddle in a minute when it's your turn,' she said firmly.

'Promise?'

'I promise. I just need to talk to Grandad for a minute.'

'Then are we going home to Nick?' Maisie asked innocently, and she heard Liz suck in her breath.

'Yes, darling, we are,' she said, and then met Liz's eyes. 'I didn't want to worry you, but when I got back to my house last Sunday the tank in the loft had been leaking and the power had cut out, so until it's all sorted it isn't safe to live there and Nick was kind enough to offer us a roof over our heads until it's fixed.'

She knew she was being hugely frugal with the truth, but the alternative was to tell her she'd been away for the weekend, and she didn't want to do that. Not in front of the children.

'Heavens! Oh, Ellie, you should have come here!'

'No,' she said firmly. 'You two had enough to worry about, and Nick's just moved into a big empty house, and he was there, and he offered, so I accepted. I didn't really have a choice, but it's been fine, really, and it's only for a little while, and we're paying him rent.'

'Are you sure? You are having the house properly looked at?' Steven asked, and she nodded.

'Oh, yes. It's being done on the insurance. David knows.'

Not that they were living with Nick, but he would now. She sighed inwardly and turned her attention to Steven, moving the attention away from Nick and back to him.

They didn't stay much longer, just long enough for her to convince him that he wasn't making a fuss or wasting anyone's time and that he couldn't afford to ignore it, and then she rounded them all up and took them home.

Well, Nick's home. Not theirs. She had to remember that, because it would be too easy to get used to it and as she'd found out last night, even he had boundaries.

Even so, it felt like home, she thought as she turned onto the drive and parked next to his car. Certainly more like home than their own did at the moment. She'd rescued what she could from the wreckage, including a lot of toys, and she was so grateful to Nick for their little playroom because it gave them somewhere to go so they weren't always in his personal space. Even if it had felt like it last night.

She was so conscious of that—maybe too conscious of it, but he hadn't had to offer them a roof over their heads and she didn't want him to end up regretting it. And a little part of her wondered if he'd suggested giving them the playroom simply *because* he wanted them out of his way. He'd certainly been happy enough to get rid of her last night.

She hadn't spoken to him since, and she was a little wary of how he'd be with her, but she needn't have worried. He appeared at the sitting room door as they went in and smiled at them as he came down to the hall.

'Hello, all. Where have you been? Have you had fun?'

'We went to see Grandad. He's got a big fat

bandage on his arm. He broke it,' Maisie said mournfully.

'Mmm. I know, I saw him when he did it.'

'I want a bandage like G'andad.'

'No, you don't,' he said to Oscar, his smile wry. 'Trust me. Broken bones aren't very comfy.'

'Why?' Oscar asked, tipping his head on one side in a gesture he'd picked up from Nick, and her heart squeezed in her chest. He would have been such a wonderful father...

'They just are. It's like if you cut yourself when you fall over, but much more sore.'

'Did you be broken?'

He nodded slowly. 'Yes, and it was very sore. It was a long time ago, though, so I'm OK now.'

Apart from the limp when he'd overdone it, and the fact that he'd never be the fantastic father he could have been if only Rachel hadn't freaked out at the thought of IVF. It must have broken his heart...

She swallowed the lump in her throat and smiled at him.

'So, how was your first Saturday morning surgery?'

'OK. No problems.' He searched her eyes. 'How's Steven? On the mend?'

'Slowly. He's seeing the cardiologist again

next week. They seem to think it was syncope, probably from arrhythmia, so they got cardiology on board. I can't believe he didn't tell Liz.'

He rolled his eyes. 'I know. It's typical, we hear it all the time. Probably too scared of what he might be told. Have you had lunch?' he asked, and she shook her head.

'No. I thought we'd go to the beach and buy some sandwiches and eat them down there. It's a gorgeous day.'

'You could come, too,' Maisie said. 'And Rufus.'

Ellie held her breath as he hesitated for a moment, then he gave her a slightly crooked smile and passed the buck.

'Your call.'

The children bounced up and down, squeaking excitedly, and Rufus rushed around and barked with delight, and she laughed and gave up trying to keep her distance.

'I think that's a yes,' she said, and met his eyes and wondered when, and how, she'd done whatever it was to deserve this man.

Except he wasn't hers, and she'd do well to remember it.

# CHAPTER NINE

THEY HAD A lovely time on the beach.

They called in at her house and rescued the windbreak and the buckets and spades from the back of the garage, and set off, armed with cheese sandwiches and bags of crisps, some fruit and a big bottle of water, and of course Rufus, who thought it was wonderful.

They built sandcastles, and dug a moat and tried to fill it with water, and then they got bored with that and dug a hole and tried to bury Nick.

And of course she had to help them, which would have been fine if it hadn't been for the way he was looking at her as she bent over him and piled sand on his chest and patted it into place.

'OK, you've got me where you want me now, what are you going to do with me?' he asked innocently, but there was nothing innocent about his eyes.

She sat back on her heels, scooped Evie onto her lap and studied him. 'I don't know. Kids, what do you think we should do to him?'

'Pour water all over him,' Maisie said, giggling, and before Ellie could stop her she picked up a bucket and ran towards the sea as she'd seen Nick do over and over again.

'Maisie, no, wait for me,' she called, but Maisie ignored her, which might have been all right if a huge wave hadn't come and knocked her off her feet.

'Maisie!'

She dumped Evie on the sand, but by the time she was on her feet Nick had pelted down the beach and into the water, but the receding wave had pulled Maisie under, and for a hideous moment Ellie was sure she was going to drown.

She didn't, but only because Nick threw himself into the surf and plucked her out of the sea. He stood up and waded out, Maisie clinging to him, and carried her gasping and sobbing up the beach to Ellie.

Speechless, she reached for her, and he put Maisie into her arms and stood there dripping, his face taut, chest heaving.

'Is she OK?'

She nodded. 'I think so. Thank you. Thank you so much. I thought…'

'I know. So did I, but she's fine.'

'Mu-Mu-Mummy,' Maisie was saying, over and over again, and Ellie held her tight and squeezed her eyes shut to stop the tears.

'Here, she's cold, aren't you, Maisie?' he said, and she felt him wrap a towel around her little girl and tuck it in. 'Come and sit down, Ellie. She'll be fine with a cuddle.'

Would she? Oh, she hoped so, because anything else was unthinkable. Her legs gave out and she sat down with a plonk on the edge of the prom and looked at the other two.

'Keep an eye on them, Nick. They move so fast.'

'I know. Don't worry, I won't let them out of my sight,' he said, with an edge to his voice that showed how worried he'd been. 'I'll pack our stuff up and we'll go home and warm up.'

She nodded, and bent and kissed her daughter's sodden hair, eyes squeezed shut against the tears of relief. She could hear Nick talking to the others, his voice cheerful and reassuring, and gradually she relaxed. Just a tiny bit.

She rocked Maisie until the shuddering stopped, and then she lifted her head and met his eyes.

'Where are the others?'

'Right behind you. We're ready to go. How is she?'

'Cold but otherwise OK, I think.'

'I can understand that. I'm freezing. I need a hot shower and I expect she does, too.' He crouched down so he was on Maisie's level and smiled at her.

'Are you OK now, poppet?'

She nodded. 'I'm—chilly,' she said, her breath still sobbing a little, and he grinned at her a bit lopsided.

'Yeah, me too. The end of April's a bit early for a dip in the sea. We might need to try again in the summer—or wear a wet suit.'

She looked at him and laughed, to Ellie's surprise. 'You're wearing a wet suit.'

He looked down and grinned at her again. 'Yes, I guess I am, sort of. Wet jeans and T-shirt, anyway. Still, it got the sand off.' He tipped his head on one side in that way of his. 'I tell you what we need to do. I think we need to go home and have a hot shower, and then make some nice rock buns and eat them while they're still warm from the oven. What do you think? Shall we go home?' he asked, holding out his hand to her, and she slipped her hand trustingly into his and slid off Ellie's lap.

He lifted her up onto the concrete walkway, picked up the bag of buckets and spades, tucked the windbreak under his arm and headed back towards the steps with Rufus at his heels, and Ellie plonked the baby on her hip and took Oscar by the hand and followed.

She watched him, the big, strong man holding her skinny little daughter's hand and smiling down at her as they walked, and her heart squeezed in her chest. It could all have been so different...

Maisie was fine after her hot shower, the incident all but forgotten, but not by Ellie.

They'd made rock buns and eaten them, played in the garden with Rufus and then gone to bed after an early supper, exhausted by the sea air and exercise.

Nick had cooked them both a meal while she'd put the children to bed and read their stories, and he was loading the dishwasher now while she wiped down the table and tried not to relive the afternoon again.

'How do you do it?' she asked, and he glanced over his shoulder at her with a puzzled frown.

'Do what?'

'Make it all seem so undramatic? One minute she's drowning, the next she wants to make rock buns.'

He smiled wryly. 'I thought she needed distracting, and I've never met a child who didn't like making and eating rock buns.'

'No, nor have I but I would never have thought of it. They were an inspired idea. Thank you—not just for that, but for saving her life. I can't thank you enough for that.' She felt her eyes fill, and blinked. 'I thought she was going to drown, Nick.'

'There were other people there on the beach, Ellie,' he said softly, 'and they were all running towards her. She wouldn't have drowned.'

'She could have done. It happens.'

'I know. But she didn't, just like the ceiling didn't fall on them. Come on, let's get a drink and go and lie down on the bed and chill for a while.'

'Not the sitting room?'

He gave her a rueful smile. 'I twanged my hip a bit leaping up, and the muscles are screaming now. I could do with a lie-down.'

She felt a wave of guilt at least as big as the wave that had knocked Maisie over. 'Oh, Nick, you should have said! You've been on your feet for hours since then, what with the baking and cooking supper and everything. Where does it hurt? Show me.'

'Oh, the usual place.'

He ran his hand down over his left buttock and thigh, and she studied him thoughtfully. He was slightly crooked, the muscles pulling him sideways a bit. They definitely needed freeing off.

'Want a massage?' she offered tentatively. 'I did a course once, when I was doing my orthopaedic rotation, and a physio showed me how. It might help.'

He gave a soft huff of laughter, and shrugged. 'You know what? That sounds amazing. I give in. Do your worst.'

*Why? Why had he let her do this?*

He turned back the duvet, lay face down on the bed in his jersey boxers and pushed them down as far as they'd go, then felt her hands on him, warm and firm and familiar, exploring his muscles, kneading his buttock gently, the flat of her palm running over his thigh.

And his body was revelling in it.

It had been a long, difficult week since they'd moved in, with her just *there* every time he turned round, sweetly scented and enticing, all mother earth and wholesome woman, and it was doing his head in. He hadn't had any respite from her at work, either, and he wanted her.

He wanted her so badly he could taste it, but he'd gritted his teeth, kept his mouth shut and his thoughts to himself, and he did it now, lying there and letting her do her worst.

And she did exactly that, with all the skill of a consummate professional, and for a moment he regretted it, but it was worth it just to have her hands on him.

Well, mostly. He let out a grunt at one point, and she apologised and eased off, but he could feel it doing him good in a fairly hideous way.

'You OK?'

'I'll live,' he said through gritted teeth. 'Just be a little careful with the scar tissue.'

'Sorry.'

'Don't be. It needs doing. I just haven't found a physio up here yet. Looks like I don't need to. You're every bit as brutal.'

She chuckled and carried on, her thumbs finding all the knots with deadly accuracy, and gradually he felt the taut muscles relax and stretch out again.

'There. I think you'll do,' she said, and then she pressed her lips fleetingly against his skin as if she was kissing it better. 'Sorry about the torture. You can get up now.'

No way. The pain had settled his libido down, but it was over now, and since he'd felt the soft warmth of her mouth against his skin his need for her was back with a vengeance.

He hoisted his underwear back up but stayed where he was. 'I think I might just lie here like this for a bit,' he said casually.

He felt the bed shift as she got off it, then the light touch of her hand on his shoulder. 'Sure. Can I get you a drink?'

*Bromide? Or maybe that malt whisky that he still hadn't found...*

'Tea would be nice.'

And it would take her a few minutes, which might give him time to get his mind sorted out and his body back in line.

To her surprise he came into the kitchen as the kettle boiled, dressed in jeans and a T-shirt and bare feet.

'Oh! You're up. I thought you were going to stay there?'

'No, I changed my mind. I feel a lot better. Thank you.'

He smiled, touched a fleeting kiss to her cheek and reached for the last of the rock buns. 'Fancy sharing?'

She laughed and shook her head. 'No way. I ate my bodyweight in them this afternoon, and we've had supper. I don't know where you put it. Right, here we go. Sitting room?'

'Mmm. Why not?' he said, and headed out of the kitchen.

She followed him up the steps, and he lay down on one of the sofas, feet crossed at the ankle, and stared up at the timber ceiling.

'What do you think I should do with those pine boards?' he mumbled through a mouthful of rock bun.

She studied them thoughtfully from the other sofa, then lay down to get a better view. 'I don't know. They're a bit orange.'

'They are, but they're iconic. It's a tough one, and it's a one-way trip.'

'But if you don't like them...?'

'I know. But what else?'

'How about colour-washing them? You know, in a sort of whitey grey wash to mute them down a bit? Sort of New England meets industrial chic?'

He chuckled, and studied them thoughtfully. 'That would work. It's a look I like. I'm going to paint the whole house white when I get round to it, and probably have neutral earthy grey carpet throughout.'

'Carpet, or wooden floors?'

'No, carpet. I don't really want wooden floors because Rufus slips on them, but apart from that I don't know what to do with it. It's early days, I suppose, and I'm still getting used to the house. Maybe I need to give it time to talk to me.'

'What, like mine, which has been shouting at me because it's so inadequate for the last four years?'

He turned his head and looked at her over his shoulder, his smile wry. 'Something like that. When do they start on yours?'

She sat up again so she could see him better. 'Monday, apparently. They pack everything and put it in storage, and it comes out when it's done, but I can get access to it if I need to. The trouble is, I need clothes for work and I haven't really got anywhere to put them, or the children's clothes. I wonder if they'd deliver my chest of drawers here? Would you mind?'

He turned his head again and looked at her as if she'd said something really weird. 'Why on earth would I mind? Of course I don't mind, but you don't need a chest of drawers, there's a spare one in the garage. We can get your stuff tomorrow if you like. I'm sure we'll find somewhere for it.'

'Are you sure? I just feel we're moving in wholesale.'

He laughed and looked away again. 'Don't be silly. Bring whatever you need. We can find room for it. The playroom's got lots of space.'

How easily he said that, as if it had always been a playroom, but she supposed it hadn't ever been anything in the three or four weeks he'd lived there before her housing crisis.

What on earth would she have done without him?

\* \* \*

'Coffee?'

She glanced up from the repeat prescriptions and smiled at Nick. 'Mmm, please. You're a saviour. I haven't had time. It was a bit of a rush, what with meeting the builders on site before I started. Thank goodness nursery could take them for longer. Oh, I've got news about Judith Granger, by the way,' she told him.

'Oh. Bad news?'

She shook her head. 'No—well, a sort of guarded no. Polyps. She's on the waiting list for a colonoscopy. They're going to remove them and send samples for histology to see if any of them have turned cancerous, so at least it's being dealt with. I should hear a few days after she has it, but I don't know when that'll be.'

He put the coffee in front of her and sat down opposite.

'So what's wrong, then?' he asked softly.

How did he know? She looked up, and he tilted his head on one side and raised an eyebrow.

She glanced across at Dev and Brian, and shook her head. 'It's not important now. Thanks for the coffee. I might go back down— I've got a few letters to write.'

He nodded and stood up. 'Yes, so have I. See you, guys.'

They walked out together, and he followed her into her room and shut the door.

'Come on, then. What is it?'

She felt her shoulders sag. 'I heard from David. He's coming up this weekend to see his parents, and obviously he wants to see the children, but they don't feel ready to have them staying there. Steven's struggling with the arrhythmia and the pain, and Liz is exhausted, so—well, I wondered if it'd be all right if they stayed with you.'

'*They*?' He looked confused. 'Where will you be?'

'Well—at yours, of course. Where else? Assuming that's all right?'

He gave a tiny huff of laughter. 'Of course it's all right. So why would it be an issue if the children stay as well?'

'Because I just don't want to take you for granted. You do so much for us, and I thought you might have been looking forward to a weekend without them.' A weekend like the others they'd shared...

He smiled, his eyes tender and a little rueful. 'I was—but not because of them. It would just be nice to spend time alone with you. I've missed it.'

'Are you sure?'

His mouth quirked a little. 'That I've missed it, or that I don't mind?'

She chuckled. 'That you don't mind.'

'Absolutely. Honestly, it's not a problem.'

She felt relief wash over her, and she smiled at him. 'Thank you.'

'You say that a lot, you know.'

'Because I mean it. I don't know what we would have done without you.'

'You would have found a way.'

He cupped her shoulders in his hands and stared down into her eyes, and then he bent his head and kissed her.

Just lightly, just enough contact to reaffirm their relationship, and then he let her go. 'I'd better get on, and so had you. I'll see you later.'

On Friday David arrived in time to pick the children up from nursery and spend the afternoon and early evening with them, so she took advantage of that to check on the builders, see what progress had been made and then blitz Nick's house while she had the chance.

She was just loading the washing machine for the second time when Nick came home, and he propped himself up against the utility room doorframe and smiled at her.

'More washing?'

'Always. It's relentless. I hate to think what it's doing to your energy bills.'

He waved a hand dismissively. 'What time are they coming back?'

'I'm picking them up at seven.'

He glanced at his watch and raised an eyebrow. 'That's in ten minutes.'

'I know. It's fine, they'll still be eating if I know them. They have a flexible attitude to bedtime, which doesn't always work with Evie.'

'Are you driving?'

'Yes. They're always tired on a Friday after nursery.' She shut the washing machine door, pressed a button and straightened up. 'Right, time to go. Our supper's in the oven, I've cleaned the sitting room and kitchen, vacuumed the bedrooms and walked Rufus round the block.'

'You're a star. Thank you.'

'Just my side of the bargain,' she said with a wry smile, and squeezed past him. Or tried to, but he caught her shoulders, pulled her up against him and kissed her.

Not like he had this morning, but that had been at work. This kiss was lingering and full of promise, and he lifted his head and gave her a wry smile.

'You'd better go and get them,' he murmured, and she nodded and walked out of the door, her lips tingling and her whole body mourning the fact that they didn't have their weekend.

To her amazement the children had finished eating when she arrived at her mother-in-law's house, so she bundled them into the car and drove straight back to Nick's. As they stepped through the front door they were bubbling over with what they'd done with their father, including a walk past her house to see how the builders were getting on, apparently, which left her mildly irritated as it was none of David's business.

Nick just raised an eyebrow, and she shrugged and chivvied them along the hall to their bedroom, Evie on her hip.

By the time they were ready for bed there was a wonderful smell coming from the kitchen. He must have taken the casserole out of the oven and checked it. It had better be ready, she was starving...

'Anybody need a bedtime story?'

'Me, me, me!' Maisie shrieked, and Ellie turned and looked up at him, standing right behind her.

'Are you volunteering?'

'It looks like it.'

She laughed softly. 'You are such a sucker.

I tell you what, why don't you read one to Maisie and Oscar, and I'll settle Evie, and then I'll read you two another story, OK?'

They nodded, delighted by the two-story promise, and as she scooped up the grizzling Evie from the floor and headed towards her room, she could hear the soft rumble of his voice and the shrill, piping clamour of their responses.

Then a laugh, and another bit of conversation, and then it all went quiet and he started to read.

'Come on, baby,' she said, picking up her bottle off the bedside table and settling down against her pillows. 'Let's read you a story, too. Shall we have this one?'

Evie snuggled down in her arms, the bottle in her mouth, but she was asleep before she was halfway down it, the story barely started.

'Poor tired baby. Have you had a busy day?' she murmured, and dropping a tender kiss on her smooth, soft brow, she eased the bottle out of her mouth and laid her carefully in her cot. She gave a tiny, sleepy cry of protest, rolled onto her front with her bottom in the air and was silent.

Ellie gave it a moment, listening to the soft sound of her breathing and the low rumble of

Nick's voice from next door, and then he said, 'The end,' very softly.

Silence.

She tiptoed out and met him in the hall, his finger on his lips. He tipped his head on one side, hands together in the prayer position under his cheek, and she nodded and slipped past him, tucked them up, kissed them both goodnight and tiptoed out again, all without disturbing them.

'They're good sleepers,' he said when she joined him in the kitchen.

'They are. It's their saving grace. Thank you for doing that. It's always a juggling act at bedtime, and I usually end up having to read two because they always want different things.'

'I got away with it lightly, then. Must be the novelty. Supper's ready, by the way. Are you hungry?'

'Starving. Let's hope it lives up to the smell.'

'It does. I tested it—well, I had to,' he said with a grin. 'It might have needed seasoning or something.'

'Yeah, right. Come on, then, let's have it. My stomach's eating itself.'

They were up with the lark in the morning, and she prised herself out of bed and went into their room and shushed them, but she needn't have bothered. Nick was already there, and he turned to her and gave her a wry grin.

'They're bright-eyed and bushy-tailed today,' he said drily, and she muffled a laugh and apologised, then kissed them both good morning.

Maisie was kneeling up on her bed and bouncing excitedly. 'Daddy said we might go to the farm park today if it's a nice day,' she said, and Ellie felt a little flicker of relief. If they were doing that, there was no chance of them popping in here on the way to or from the beach, which meant they'd have privacy. She just hoped the weather played ball.

Nick obviously clocked that, too, and he opened the curtains and one of his eyebrows twitched. 'Well, it's a lovely day,' he said with a smile. 'What time are you dropping them off?'

'Nine o'clock. Why?'

'Perfect. We'll have time to walk Rufus round the block before you go. You like that, don't you, guys?'

'Can I hold his lead?' Maisie asked, and Oscar immediately said he wanted to, and if Nick hadn't calmly intervened there would have been a riot.

'You can take turns. And don't start argu-ing about who's going first, we'll toss a coin.'

'What's that mean?' Maisie asked.

'Get dressed nicely for Mummy, and I'll show you. I'm going to have a shower.'

Twenty minutes later they were gathered in the kitchen, and he was showing them a coin.

'OK, so that's the head, and that's the tail.'

'But it hasn't got a tail,' Maisie said, as if she suddenly didn't believe a word he said.

'Ah, well. Look at Rufus. What's at this end?' He swivelled the dog round so he was facing them.

'His head.'

He turned him back again. 'And this end?'

'That's his tail.'

'Exactly. The coin is the same. There's a head on one side, so the other side's called the tail.'

'But it doesn't *have* a tail,' Maisie said again, with that stubborn look on her face he was beginning to recognise, and out of the corner of his eye he could see Ellie, hand over her mouth, eyes creased with laughter.

'I know. Silly, isn't it? But it doesn't matter, because we know that, and so long as we can tell the difference that's all that matters.'

'But why does it matter?'

'Because,' he said, picking up the coin and flicking it into the air, 'when it lands, it's got to be one way up or the other, and if it's the one you chose, then you win.'

'Why?' they chorused, and he gave up.

'I tell you what,' he said, utterly exasperated, 'whoever's ready at the door first with their shoes on has the first go. Deal?'

Ellie dropped the children off promptly at nine, armed with sun cream, wellies and strict instructions to wash their hands after they touched any of the animals, and she went back, walked through the front door and straight into Nick's arms.

He gave her a hug, then lifted his head and looked down into her eyes.

'Well, we're alone. What now?'

She smiled wryly. 'Coffee? We should give them half an hour or so to realise they've forgotten something. And anyway, I could do with one. It's been a long old week.'

'Tell me about it. Cappuccino?'

'Perfect. We can drink it in the garden. It's gorgeous out there, it seems a shame not to soak it up.'

They went out with their coffees and sat on the bench in the sunshine, faces turned up to the sun.

'This is so nice' she sighed. 'I love this garden. There's always somewhere shady and somewhere sunny, no matter what time of day. I do envy you. Mine's in deep shade all morning and full sun all afternoon.'

'How's the building work coming on? You mentioned it last night but you didn't say a lot.'

'Oh, it's gutted, all the back half. I didn't really recognise it, but the site foreman was on the phone so I couldn't talk to him about timescales or anything, which was a bit frustrating, but they're certainly getting on with it. The skip was full of kitchen, I know that. We could take a wander round there later, have a closer look.'

'Have you decided what you're doing with it?'

'No. I think a quick fix and put it on the market, to be honest. It's just not big enough, and after being here, seeing how the children love to run around in the bigger garden, having the luxury of a playroom and a utility room instead of the washing machine in the garage—well, it's just pointed out all its failings, really, and they were bad enough before.'

'Can you afford to move?'

'Oh, yes. I don't have a mortgage, don't forget, so I should be able to upgrade if I don't go mad.'

'You'll lose your sea views.'

She laughed. 'Well, you know how much

that bothers me,' she said, smiling up at him, and then she felt her smile fade as she read the look in his eyes.

'Come to bed,' he murmured softly.

'What, in broad daylight?' she teased, and he grinned.

'There's nothing in the rules that says it needs to be dark.' His smile faded, his eyes intent. 'I just need to hold you.'

She lifted a hand and cradled his jaw, feeling the prickle of stubble against her palm. 'That's a shame,' she murmured. 'I was hoping for rather more than that.'

He gave a soft huff of laughter and pulled her to her feet.

'I can't tell you how happy that makes me...'

# CHAPTER TEN

THEY WENT FOR a walk later, to see her house.

It was the first time he'd seen it since it had been emptied, and now it was gutted it seemed small and cramped and sadder than ever. And noisy, with the roar of the industrial dehumidifiers in the background.

They went out to the garden so they could hear themselves think, and from out there he could see it wasn't possible to do all the things she'd said she'd like to do.

'There isn't really any way to make it work, is there? No easy way, and you'll never be able to make the garden bigger.'

'No. No, I won't. It isn't big enough to do anything significant with, but it'll do until I find somewhere better to go.'

Somewhere like his?

He felt an odd tug in his gut, a fierce longing, and suppressed it. 'Have you chosen the kitchen units?'

'No. I've got a brochure. I need to do it by Monday, I think.'

She looked dispirited, and he slung his arm around her shoulders and gave her a quick hug.

'Come on, let's go and get Rufus and take him somewhere nice for lunch, a pub with a garden. Got any suggestions?'

'There's a pub on the other side of the river that's supposed to be nice. I know the way.'

That day set the tone for the next two weekends when David came up.

Ellie kept the children overnight, he had them in the day, and she and Nick spent those precious days together in what she'd come to think of as their fantasy bubble.

And all the time her house was nearing completion.

So was work on the medical centre, and they moved into the new downstairs staff room with brand-new, comfy furniture and a decent coffee machine, which made Nick happy. She found out that Judith Granger didn't have cancer, to her relief and Ellie's, and she was less stressed about work because Liz was able to help again with the children from time to time as Steven's heart seemed stable on his new drug regime.

Not so hers.

Living with Nick, listening to him interacting with the children, listening to the children playing with Rufus in the garden, lying on the sofas at night and staring at the ceiling and talking about not a lot, not to mention the days they spent together when David was there for the weekend—it was like living out a dream, and when her house was finished she'd have to go home and stop playing Happy Families with a man who'd only taken them all on out of the kindness of his too-generous heart.

He never complained, but then he never had, to the point that he'd had to take drastic action to get his parents to notice that he was struggling, and the last thing she wanted was to put him in that position again, so as soon as her house was ready, they'd move back.

But for now they were where they were, so she still had a little more time, and she tried not to think about it.

And then, long before she was ready, the house was. Or almost. It was David's last weekend before she moved back in, and she spent those two days unpacking all the things that had been put in storage and putting them away, making up the beds in readiness in bedrooms that smelt of fresh paint and new carpet. All that remained was plumbing in the sink and the new dishwasher and washing machine on Monday, and she could move in, so she went back to Nick's and started to sort out the things they had there.

She was packing up the toys in the 'playroom' that really wasn't, when he came in and sat down on the sofa, studying her thoughtfully.

'What time are you picking them up?'

'Five. Why?'

He looked at his watch. 'So we've got two hours. Come to bed with me, Ellie.'

She looked away, her throat working, unable to hold his eyes. 'I don't think we should.'

'Why? You've been avoiding me all weekend. I don't understand. Have I done something wrong?'

'No! No, of course not. It's just…' She shrugged helplessly. 'I'm not sure it's a good idea. Not now.'

'Why? Why should it suddenly not be a good idea?'

She looked back at him, feeling a little desperate.

*Because every time we make love, I fall a little deeper in love with you, and it's killing me.*

'Because we've invaded your space for

weeks now, and I'm so conscious of taking advantage of your good nature, and I really don't want to do anything to make it any more difficult for us all when we move back out.'

'How will it make it more difficult?'

'Because I don't honestly know *what* I feel for you, and every time we make love, it confuses me even more. Yes, I care, but I also feel a huge amount of gratitude, and obviously sexual attraction, that goes without saying, but I don't know if it's more than that, and I don't know if you really want us or if you're only doing it because that's what you do, take on lame ducks and look after them. You've done it all your life, and here I am, another lame duck with a whole brood of baby ducklings all needing your help, and the closer we are to each other, the harder it is to know what's real and what's just wishful thinking.'

'Oh, Ellie. Come here.' He sighed and reached for her, getting to his feet, but she held up her hands.

'Please, Nick. Don't touch me. Don't make it impossible for me to do this. I have to do this my way. It's not that I don't want you...'

He dropped his hands and took a step back, and he looked confused but resigned.

'OK. If that's how you feel, then I respect

that. And of course we don't have to do anything you don't want to do. The last thing I want is for you to stay with me out of *gratitude.*' He glanced at his watch, and opened the door. 'I need to walk Rufus. I'll see you later.'

He didn't understand.

Why would she feel like that? He could understand where she was coming from, but really? *Gratitude?* Surely to God it was more than that? He shook his head, not sure whether to feel rejected or not, but it nagged at him as he walked.

Was she right about him? About him taking lame ducks under his wing and looking after them? Was that all it was, him falling back into familiar habits? Because it didn't feel like that. Maybe she was right, maybe they were too close.

But he wanted to be close to her, and he was pretty damn sure she wanted to be close to him. Or she had.

What had changed?

And then Rufus sat down and refused to move, and he realised he'd been walking for two hours.

His ankle was killing him, his hip was aching, and there was no way on God's earth he was asking Ellie for a massage.

He looked around and realised he had no idea where he was, so he got his phone out and pulled up a map.

Three streets away, buried in the back of the housing development behind her house. He must have walked round in a circle. Just like his mind.

He hobbled slowly back with the reluctant dog, and she was just getting the children out of the car when he arrived home.

She gave him a sharp look and frowned.

'Are you OK? You've been ages.'

She sounded worried, so he dredged up a smile and tried not to limp.

'Of course I'm all right, I've been exploring.'

'You're limping.'

'Only a bit. I got a bit lost and overdid it.'

He looked away and smiled at the children as they ran towards him, little Evie taking a few tentative steps before sitting down with a plop.

'Hey, you're walking, clever girl!' he said, and scooped her up without thinking and carried her inside, and she snuggled into his neck and patted his face.

'Nick,' she said, as clear as day, and he had to swallow hard. God, he loved her. Loved them all. When had that happened? Ellie was right, it was going to be impossibly hard when they moved back into their house in the next few days, and he was going to miss them unbearably.

*How did I let this happen?*

'We went to Southwold and had too much ice cream and Oscar was sick in Daddy's car,' Maisie told him, getting down on the floor in the hall and cuddling the exhausted Rufus, and he had to remind himself that what their father chose to feed them was none of his business. And anyway, who was he to criticise? He'd nearly walked the dog off his legs.

'I bet that didn't make him very happy,' he said, and Maisie giggled.

'He was very cross.'

'Well, it serves him right,' Ellie said. 'He shouldn't have given you so much ice cream. He knows Oscar gets carsick sometimes. Right, come on, time for supper and an early night. You've got nursery at eight tomorrow.'

She didn't know how she got through the evening.

Nick was obviously sore, but she didn't dare suggest giving him a massage, not after what she'd said, and as soon as they'd eaten in a rather strained silence she made the excuse of needing to pack a few more things and took herself off to give him space.

He seemed—well, she didn't know what he seemed.

Hurt? Angry? Confused?

All of the above, perhaps, and she felt awful, but she'd also felt that she was being sucked inexorably into a delusion of happiness that probably wasn't real. How could it be? She hardly knew him.

So she shut herself away in the playroom and sorted out more of their things, folded washing, had a shower and dried her hair and got everything ready for the morning.

She heard him go out with Rufus for the last time, and went into the kitchen, made herself a drink and took it to her room, closing the door firmly.

A few minutes later she heard him walk down the corridor and pause by her room. She held her breath, her heart pounding, and then he went past and she heard the slight creak of his bedroom door, the click of a light switch, the sound of running water.

She let out her breath and felt the tension drain out of her. She felt sick. Sick that she'd destroyed the dream, taken it away from both of them, but it was only that, a dream.

Wasn't it?

So why did it hurt so much?

*Please let the plumber come tomorrow. I need to go home...*

They moved out the following day.

The plumber had been, she said, and so she left the children with Liz and went back to his house to get the last of their things.

She was there when he got back, ferrying stuff out to her car, and she put the things in the boot and closed the lid, then turned to him.

'I think that's everything,' she said, and her voice sounded tight and strained and maybe a little tearful. 'I'll just have a last check round.'

He followed her in and sat on the bottom of the stairs, Rufus at his feet having his ears fondled and watching her every move. He heard her go into the utility room, heard the sound of the tumble dryer start, and then she reappeared.

'I've put the bedding on to dry,' she said. 'I washed it this morning. I think I've got everything now, but if I haven't—'

'I'll take it to work.'

'Thank you.'

Her voice was small and sad, and he wanted to cry for her. For her, for him, for the children.

He got to his feet, his ankle still sore from

yesterday, and for a moment they just stood there facing each other, neither of them sure what to do.

She broke first, and as she took a step towards him he reached for her, folding her against his chest and gritting his teeth. Don't go, he wanted to say, but he didn't, because he knew she would whatever he said, and he knew he had to let her go if that was what she really wanted. She needed to know how she felt, needed space to do that, and maybe he did, too.

'I'll miss you,' he told her gruffly, and she nodded.

'I'll miss you, too,' she said, her voice clogged with tears. 'Thank you so, so much for all you've done for us. I have no idea what we would have done without you.'

'You would have coped. You're strong, Ellie. You don't need me, or not for that. It just made it a little easier for you, that's all.' He dropped his arms and stepped away from her, and it felt as if he was tearing his heart out.

'You'd better go, it's getting late,' he said, his voice scratchy and rough, and she nodded and picked her bag up off the floor.

'Your keys,' she said, and held them out to him.

He took them carefully, without touching

her fingers, because he knew if he touched her again he wouldn't be able to let her go, and then he stood back and watched as she got in her car and drove away.

Then he closed the door, went into the kitchen and the first thing he saw was the pictures plastered all over the fridge. He laid his hand over Evie's tiny handprint, and had to swallow hard.

No. He wasn't going to do this. He was *not* going to cry.

He wrenched open the fridge door, poured himself a glass of wine and took it into the playroom.

*The playroom.*

He looked around, hearing the children's voices in his head, their laughter, tears, squabbles, the shrill chatter, the endless 'Why's from Oscar. He heard Ellie's voice yesterday, begging him to let her do it her way.

He couldn't stay in there, so he went up to the sitting room and lay on the sofa, staring at the ceiling.

*You could colourwash it... New England meets industrial chic...*

He swore and sat up, turned on the television and ignored it, like he ignored the wine.

Rufus came and got on his lap, looking forlorn, and licked his face and barked softly.

'Oh, Rufus. Are you hungry?' he asked, and took him down and fed him, but the dog turned away from the bowl.

She'd probably fed him.

He opened the fridge again without looking at the pictures and stared at the contents without any real interest. He had to eat something. Cheese?

He made a cheese sandwich, and it reminded him instantly of the night she'd found the leak, lying on his bed with her eating sandwiches and listening for the sound of the children if they woke and were disorientated.

And the picnic on the beach, when Maisie had nearly drowned.

He went out into the garden, sitting in the twilight with his sandwich and the glass of wine, and he could hear the sound of the children again.

A dog barked in the distance, but Rufus ignored it, lying on his feet and looking forlorn. The dog had followed him everywhere he'd gone to try and escape the memories, but he couldn't, because their presence was everywhere, in every nook and cranny of the house.

So he gave up, the wine untouched, the sandwich half-eaten, and got into the bed where he'd made love to her so many times.

Not a huge improvement.

He stared up at the ceiling and wondered why a woman he hadn't even known three months ago could make him feel so lost and so alone. So rejected, for heaven's sake.

He thought back over all the things she'd said over the past few weeks, trying to work out when she'd changed. Or maybe she hadn't. Maybe he'd just ignored the signals.

She'd jumped at the idea of the playroom, and according to her it was always a question of keeping out of his hair and giving him his space, but was that simply because she herself had needed her own space? Saying it was for him, when really it was for her?

Maybe he *should* be feeling rejected. Maybe he'd taken too much for granted, assumed that they'd want him in their life as much as he'd finally realised he wanted them in his? Was she just protecting the children? He could understand that, but it didn't surely mean they couldn't still carry on as they had before? Did they have to lose everything they'd had in order to protect the children?

He had no idea, but he knew he couldn't solve this on his own. They should be talking. Properly talking, so they both knew where they were coming from.

Except not now. She needed time to find out how she really felt, something she obviously felt she hadn't been able to do while she was still living with him and had no easy options, and maybe he did, too, so now probably wasn't the best time to tackle it. No, if that was what she wanted, he'd go along with it and wait, give her the time she'd asked for.

It was hardly going to kill him.

It didn't feel like home.

It should, because nothing about it had really changed, but in a weird way it was completely different. It reminded her of when she'd gone home from uni and her father's wife—not her stepmother, she could never bring herself to think of her as that—had gone through the house from end to end and eradicated all that was familiar.

Which was ridiculous, because everything about the bits that had been changed—the carpets, the colour of the walls, the kitchen units and appliances—all of it had been her choice.

And yet it felt like a rental. An inadequate rental.

It didn't help that the children were so unhappy, either. She'd thought they'd be pleased, but Evie had taken ages to settle in her cot, and Maisie had cried herself to sleep because she missed Nick.

They'd had a special bond since he'd rescued her from the sea, and she'd wrenched them apart without giving the children time to say goodbye. That had probably been unfair, but she'd been unable to do it without breaking down, and anyway he'd gone to work that morning before she'd had the call from the plumber to say he was going in, so she hadn't really had a chance.

She got out of bed in the dark and stood at the open window, listening to the quiet sound of the sea, the barking of a dog, the hoot of an owl. Was it the one she'd heard from his house? Possibly. He wasn't far away. A car drove past slowly, and she wondered hopefully if it was Nick, but it wasn't.

She got back into bed and tried not to think about him, but it was impossible. She could feel his arms around her, his mouth on her, their bodies so in tune. Hear his voice so clearly as he'd reached out to her just yesterday afternoon.

*Come to bed with me, Ellie...*

And she'd turned him down, so it wouldn't hurt, and now she regretted it because they could have had that one last bitter-sweet time together before the dream was over.

Because it couldn't be real. She'd only met him at the end of March, and it was still only

June. How *could* it be real? That sort of thing only happened in books.

No, it was gratitude, and honeymoon sex. A dangerous combination.

Time to get back to reality, however stark it was.

Nick stuck it out for two weeks before he cracked.

In that fortnight, he went through the house and cleaned it to within an inch of its life. Not that it needed it, because she'd pretty much kept it clean, but he pulled out all the furniture and found a toy and a T-shirt of Maisie's with unicorns on the front that made him want to cry.

She loved her unicorn T-shirt so much...

And then he went into the playroom, but it was too sad and empty, barren now without the clutter of multicoloured plastic toys that had filled it until so recently, so that weekend he found the shelving unit he'd brought from the house in Bath, rebuilt it in the playroom and then tackled the stack of boxes one by one, starting with the stuff from his old house, which he'd never had time to deal with.

He found a few things worth keeping, but all the rest he took to the dump or charity shops. Most of it meant nothing, or at least nothing he wanted to remember. He didn't need mementos of a broken marriage, and this was long overdue.

And then the following weekend he tackled Sam's possessions, and it tore him apart.

Or maybe he was already torn apart and it just set his emotions free.

He found all sorts of things—a postcard of the seaside town they'd visited the last time he and Sam had gone to the beach, with a photograph of him and Sam on the sand, and a half-eaten stick of peppermint rock, bright pink on the outside, white inside with the name of the town running down the core in bright pink letters. They'd had an amazing day. He'd lifted Sam out of his wheelchair and dug a hole in the sand and propped him up in it so he could be comfortable on the beach, and he'd buried his legs, just like the children had buried him in the sand.

And Sam had laughed until the tears had run down his face.

They'd stayed there until he was too cold, and then they'd gone and found a stall selling rock, and he'd unwrapped it for Sam and he'd sucked the end of it and said it was the best thing he'd ever tasted.

Sam had insisted on keeping it, smelling it

every now and then to remind him of that day. Did it still smell?

He lifted it out of the box and unwrapped the end carefully, peeling the Cellophane away from the sticky sweet, and he sniffed it and smiled. It did. Only faintly now, but enough to remind him, and he closed the Cellophane wrapper and laid it gently back in the box next to the photograph and the postcard, and opened another box.

Photos in this one, lots of them, including a photo of them taken after his accident, in matching wheelchairs.

And the last photo of Sam, with Rufus lying by his side, shortly before he died.

The image blurred, and he blinked and swiped his cheeks with the back of his hand, laid the photo back in the box and closed the lid.

So many memories, so many happy times.

And they *had* been happy. It wasn't all about the sad stuff. He'd forgotten how good it was, how much fun they'd had. It had taken him all this time to realise it, but he'd been happy with Sam, and Sam had been happy, too, and despite all the problems he'd loved Sam with all his heart and wouldn't have changed a thing. Why had he never realised this before?

He packed it all away again. He'd go through

it later with his family, when they were ready, because he knew it would be good for them to do it, but not yet. They weren't ready yet, but he had been, and he'd seen enough for now.

Enough to know that Ellie was wrong about him. It wasn't about lame ducks, it was about unconditional love, the love he'd felt for Sam, for his sisters, for his parents. The love he felt for her and her children, and he needed to tell her that.

He looked at his watch.

Midday. Would she be at home? He knew David was up this weekend, he'd heard her mention it in the staff room. Not that she'd told him. They were walking carefully round each other, treading on eggshells, and the atmosphere between them was strained to say the least.

Time to change that, to clear the air if nothing else.

He'd given her long enough.

She ought to make herself some lunch. She couldn't really be bothered, but it might make a change from moping around the house and wallowing in self-pity.

She went into her new kitchen and looked at the fridge. It was blank, because she'd left the pictures behind.

Had he thrown them out? He didn't need to, they weren't that precious. The children painted things at nursery all the time. She'd soon get more. But she could still see him laying his hand over Evie's handprint, see the look on his face, that touch of sorrow.

*He should have been a father...*

She pulled out cheese and butter, found a couple of slices of bread and made a cheese sandwich, but it reminded her of the beach, the day that Maisie had nearly drowned.

If he hadn't been there...

There was a knock on the door, and she put the sandwich down and went to open it.

'Nick?'

'Can we talk?'

She searched his eyes, serious but determined, and she shrugged and stepped back, letting him in.

'Coffee?'

'No. I want to take you somewhere. I've got something to show you, something that might solve your housing crisis.'

She studied him, but he was giving nothing away. 'Really? Because I went and looked at a house this morning and it was awful. So where is this house? Who's it on the market with?'

'It isn't at the moment, although it was. It's word of mouth.'

'Oh. Right.' Now she was intrigued, but only vaguely, because having him here in her house made her realise that all she needed was him, and she didn't know how to start that conversation.

'Shall we go?'

'Um—yes, OK. Is it far away? Are we driving?'

'No, I thought we could walk.'

'OK.' She picked up her keys, checked the windows were shut and set the alarm, closing the door behind her. 'So where are we going?'

'Just down here.'

They turned into Jacob's Lane, and her feet slowed to a halt.

'Nick…'

He turned to face her, his eyes more open and honest than she'd ever seen them.

'Hear me out, Ellie. We need to talk. There's so much we've left unsaid, so much we should have opened up about. You owe us that much. I owe us that much.'

She hesitated, but his gaze didn't waver, his eyes fixed on hers, so transparent now. She could read the love in them, read the hurt, read the willingness to listen. And so she nodded and went with him.

He opened the front door and ushered her

in, closing it softly behind her, and Rufus ran to her, tail wiggling furiously.

'Hello, sweetie,' she said, crouching down and hugging him, but Nick was waiting.

'Come with me,' he said, and then he took her by the hand and led her through towards the playroom.

No, it wasn't the playroom, she couldn't call it that—and anyway, he went straight past it, down to the end, to his room. What was he doing?

'So, this is the master bedroom suite,' he said, and the penny dropped. 'It has plenty of storage, and a walk-in shower big enough for two.'

She remembered that only too well.

He opened the patio door and beckoned her out. 'It leads out into the garden, which I understand from a friend has sunshine and shade in some part or another all day long. It's totally enclosed, so it's child- and dog-friendly, it's got enough room for them to run about, corners for den building, and yet it's manageable. There's room over there for a new garage, so the existing garage could be turned into a playroom or games room. It needs a bigger paved area for family seating, but that could be done,' he added, and led her back inside.

'This is the second bedroom, with two more

of very similar size, and a family bathroom here, which ideally could be refitted. And this is a very useful utility room with space for everything you might need, and a door to the garden.'

She shook her head and followed him, knowing exactly what he was up to but hearing him out because, as he'd pointed out, they owed each other that.

'Right, the kitchen. The proper dining table at the moment is in the hall, but there's room to extend the kitchen forward to make a bigger kitchen dining room, and then up here is the sitting room. It could do with updating. A good friend suggested New England meets industrial chic might work quite well.'

He turned and met her eyes as they got to the top of the stairs, and his smile was gentle.

'Am I a good friend?' she asked, a lump in her throat, and he nodded.

'I think so. Don't you?'

She looked up at the ceiling, blinking hard. 'Nick, what are you getting at? I need to know.'

'You do. Sit down. This could take a while.'

He reached for a box, a small cardboard box with a lid, and he sat beside her, took the lid off and handed her a photograph.

'Who's this?'

'Samuel. Here's another one of both of us,

taken on the same day. It was the last time we ever went to the beach together. It must have been about five or six years ago. We had a wonderful day. We laughed the whole time, and I treasure that memory.'

She stared at the photo of him and his brother, so alike in many ways and yet so different.

'Here's another one. This is after my accident—I had a wheelchair for a while, so for that time we were the same, Sam and I. He teased me mercilessly about my incompetence with it, but his was electric so it was easier for him.'

He was smiling, his face an echo of happy memories, and he took the photos back from her and handed her another one, his smile fading. 'This was just before he died, about eighteen months ago, with Rufus.'

'Gosh, he looks so different.' She traced her finger over his face, ravaged by illness, his eyes vacant now, one hand lying over his faithful dog.

Her eyes welled with tears, and she handed it back and looked away, sucking in a breath.

'You don't need to cry for him, Ellie. It was a happy release, and we've all shed enough tears. Rufus cried for weeks, and so did we, me and my parents and my sisters, but that's over now. It's time to remember the good things, and there were so many.'

'I thought you resented him?'

He nodded. 'So did I. I've spent years thinking he was a burden, feeling resentful, but actually I just felt guilty because I was all right and he wasn't. Looking back on it, we were happy, Sam and I. We had a good childhood, although it was very different to what it would have been. But it didn't cost me my marriage. My marriage was a mistake, based on a whole lot of assumptions about how much I could ask of a woman who really had no idea what she was taking on.'

'In what way?'

He shrugged. 'My commitment to Sam, to my parents. My inability to give her the children she wanted without going through the process of IVF, which she really didn't want to do. It wasn't fair to expect Rachel to accept all that, but it did point up what was missing between us. We didn't love each other unconditionally. If we had, we might have made it, and I regret that, but it wasn't Sam's fault, it was mine.

'I thought I'd given up a lot to be with Sam, but actually I didn't give up anything worth having because my marriage was already broken. Sharing my time with him, caring for him, being with him taught me a lot about myself, gave me far more back than I gave him, and it hasn't held me back in any way. I've done what I wanted to, achieved what I set out to achieve, and I'm a good doctor, a fairly decent human being, I think, and I'm where I want to be. Or I was, until I met you, and then it all changed.'

'Changed?'

She searched his eyes, and he smiled tenderly.

'Yes, it changed. It was like opening a window on a part of me I hadn't known existed, and letting in the sunshine. I'd never dared to imagine living in a family, not after Rachel pulled the plug on our IVF plans. I'd put it all aside, and I thought I'd accepted it, but suddenly there you were with your beautiful little children, and I realised what I'd been missing. All that warmth and joy that I hadn't appreciated when I was young suddenly made sense.'

'So that was the draw?' she asked, feeling hollowed out inside to know that it was only the children, but he shook his head fiercely.

'No! No, that wasn't the draw, you were. You, with your warmth and kindness and sense of mischief, your humour, your incredible sensuality—the kids were a drawback, Ellie. I didn't think I wanted to have anything to do with you because of them, but then you lost your home and I rashly opened the doors to you and in came the sunlight. Not a burden to be carried, but a joy.'

'Not always.'

'No, of course not, but they are a joy, and I love them. I love them dearly. I love you dearly, but I don't *need* you, any of you. I have a life I'm happy with, I'm reasonably self-sufficient—I can live without you, just as you can live without me. You're strong and clever and resourceful, you've made a home for your children that might not be perfect but that works perfectly well enough for now, and you're an excellent doctor, a caring and decent human being, and you've made a success of your life, just as I have.

'But it isn't what I *want*. What I *want* is you, Ellie. I love you. I love you so much, and I can't tell you how much I've missed you, but if you come back to me, then don't do it out of gratitude, don't do it because you feel sorry for me or guilty, do it because you love me, too, and you want to be with me for ever, unconditionally. Because this is the deal. If you come back to me, I want it to be as my wife, so don't do it if you can't buy into that, because I'd rather lose you now than down the line when it'll hurt all of us much, much more.'

Ellie stared at him, letting his words sink in, and she felt a bubble of something wonderful bursting in her chest.

'I do need you. I've missed you so much. I haven't been able to eat, or sleep, or think— I thought, if I went home, I'd be able to see more clearly, but all I could see was that I was wrong, and I'm so, so sorry.'

She reached out and cradled his jaw in her hand, feeling the muscles jump beneath her thumb, and she smiled at him sadly.

'I love you, Nick. I love you so much. I didn't dare believe in it, I thought it was too quick to be real, but I was wrong, wasn't I? Because it is real, it isn't a dream. We did fall in love. I love you more than I ever thought I could love anyone. I just didn't know how to tell you, or if you'd want to hear it.'

'Is that a yes?'

She laughed, but it cracked in the middle and she reached for him at the same time as he reached for her.

'Yes, it's a yes,' she said, and he gathered her up against his chest and held her so tight she thought her ribs would crack.

'Thank you.'

She eased away and looked up at him again. 'Don't thank me, Nick. You've given me so much. You've given me back my faith in love, my ability to trust. I can't tell you how much that means to me. And—I've been thinking. You know how you talked about IVF, how it might be possible for you to have a baby that way?'

He looked away. 'I don't need a baby, Ellie. You've got three beautiful children, and I already love them. Why would I need more?'

'I don't know. Maybe because I do? Maybe because I want to carry your child, if I can?'

He looked back at her, his eyes bright. He blinked hard and sucked in a breath. 'You'd do that for me? It's not easy, Ellie. IVF is tough.'

'I know. But I've sailed through every pregnancy and delivery, I think I can tolerate a little bit of tough for something so important.'

He shook his head, disbelief in his eyes, and maybe the dawning of hope? 'I'm nearly forty-one, Ellie. I've survived this long without my own children.'

'No. You've put away hope. You don't have to do that any more, not if you don't want to.'

'I can't believe you'd do that for me,' he said, his voice cracking, and she felt her eyes welling with tears.

'I love you, Nick. Why wouldn't I? And I'm only thirty-five. We've still got time. Let's see how it goes, eh? Just leave it there for now.'

'It's not a deal breaker?'

'Of course it's not a deal breaker. It's an offer, that's all. A part of my unconditional love for you.'

He was silent for an age, and then he nodded. 'OK. We'll think about it. And—more importantly, how about your children? How will they take this? Will they accept me?'

'Accept you?' She laughed softly, her eyes welling again. 'They haven't stopped begging to see you again since we moved out. Maisie cries herself to sleep, Oscar talks all the time about Rufus, and every time the doorbell rings they look hopeful.'

She took his hand. 'They miss you, Nick. I miss you. We just want to come home.'

# EPILOGUE

THE APRIL SUN was warm on their faces as they sat in the garden, watching the children play.

They were running around on the grass with Rufus, their happy laughter filling the air, and Nick looked down at her and smiled.

'Happy?'

'Of course I'm happy. You?'

'What do you think? I reckon it's all going perfectly.'

It was. David had bought her old house as a base for his weekends now he was bringing his pilot girlfriend with him and wanted privacy, and they were planning to use the money on Nick's house. Especially now…

'So, how do you feel about starting that extension?' he asked. 'We'll need another bedroom soon, and the garage needs to be a playroom before the winter. Can you stand it?'

'I should think so. We can always ship the children out to David and Ava. She loves having them and he's so much more reasonable now. I never thought that would ever happen.'

He gave a chuckle, then lifted her hand to his lips, pressing a kiss to her wedding ring before laying his hand over the smooth curve of their baby. 'I never thought this would, either. I can't believe it.'

She laughed softly. 'I can. I'd forgotten about morning sickness, but at least it's over.'

He laughed and hugged her closer against his side, his arm around her shoulders.

'I'm so glad. I wonder what the children will make of him?'

'They'll be delighted. Maisie was thrilled when Evie was born, and Oscar will be so happy to have a brother.' She looked up at him. 'Can we call him Samuel?'

His eyes were suddenly bright, his smile a little crooked as he bent his head and kissed her.

'I think that would be wonderful…'

* * * * *

*If you enjoyed this story, check out
these other great reads from
Caroline Anderson*

**From Heartache to Forever
A Single Dad to Heal Her Heart
One Night, One Unexpected Miracle
Their Own Little Miracle**

*All available now!*